Shepherds Awake

DAVID SARLES

WESTBOW PRESS
A DIVISION OF THOMAS NELSON
& ZONDERVAN

Copyright © 2014 David Sarles.

All rights reserved. No part of this book may be used or reproduced by any means, graphic, electronic, or mechanical, including photocopying, recording, taping or by any information storage retrieval system without the written permission of the publisher except in the case of brief quotations embodied in critical articles and reviews.

WestBow Press books may be ordered through booksellers or by contacting:

WestBow Press
A Division of Thomas Nelson & Zondervan
1663 Liberty Drive
Bloomington, IN 47403
www.westbowpress.com
1 (866) 928-1240

Because of the dynamic nature of the Internet, any web addresses or links contained in this book may have changed since publication and may no longer be valid. The views expressed in this work are solely those of the author and do not necessarily reflect the views of the publisher, and the publisher hereby disclaims any responsibility for them.

Any people depicted in stock imagery provided by Thinkstock are models, and such images are being used for illustrative purposes only.
Certain stock imagery © Thinkstock.

ISBN: 978-1-4908-4402-2 (sc)
ISBN: 978-1-4908-4874-7 (e)

Library of Congress Control Number: 2014912158

Printed in the United States of America.

WestBow Press rev. date: 8/20/2014

Contents

Preface vii

I 1
II 4
III 6
IV 12
V 17
VI 20
VII 26
VIII 31
IX 36
X 41
XI 48
XII 52
XIII 56
XIV 61
XV 66
XVI 73
XVII 81
XVIII 87
XIX 92
XX 96
XXI 101
XXII 105
XXIII 110
XXIV 115
XXV 120

XXVI	125
XXVII	131
XXVIII	138
XXIX	144
XXX	151
XXXI	156
XXXII	159
XXXIII	162

Preface

OLD FAMILY STORIES morph with retelling and tend towards epic and legend. Everyday events gain historic proportions. Ordinary people emerge through portals as immortal beings with unusual powers of dominance.

King David is immortalized for slaying a giant. Before that he was a shepherd. Before he composed a hundred some Psalms, he was only a better than average music student.

As it is passed down through my father's line, the story of a somewhat-less-famous-than-David shepherd, last name of Sarles, dragged a flock of sheep across New York State and states west to Boscobel, Wisconsin. So it is said. He only stopped there, it seems, because the Mississippi River was at floodstage, or simply running too fast. Or more likely, he was done in.

Along comes his ancestor, Cousin Florence, who said, as a girl she went to the family house in Boscobel and woke up one morning to a Native American face staring through her bedroom window.

She would have invited him in for tea, I thought, except probably the other members of the household were not up yet. She did, however, invite my new girlfriend and me for Sunday afternoon tea and stories. Over tea and water biscuits she told us of her Boscobel, Wisconsin trip.

My girlfriend, only our second time ever on a date, and I corralled a runaway horse that stopped traffic on the Hutchinson Parkway on our drive to see Cousin Florence. We arrived slightly disheveled. My cousin had the brilliance to ask me and my date, "When are you two going to be married?"

Now it's our story.

Dedicated to the memory of Florence Sarles Durston Hamilton

I

There had been no rain this month nor the last. The sun browned the grass leading to the river. Only the grasses along the shore of the Hudson past the railroad tracks down to Esopus Creek grew green, and our sheep worked along through the grasses until the railroad chuffed back along the tracks evenings. Our dogs would chase the sheep up into our pasture through black smoke of the locomotive.

John Dark Sky drew the course of the Hudson River in the dirt road with a stick. His map of the river and the canal was etched in a baked roadpath. The road led down through our pasture past Uncle Peter's pasture to the Hudson River. John Dark Sky scraped a straight line to show the river's course and broken lines for the canal to the west of Albany. "Here. The flatboat canal." And he scored the dry roadbed with a W. And below the mark, "Here are lakes like fingers." He held his brown hand fanned out touching the earth beneath the lines.

"My father was much like your father, Jesse," John Dark Sky said. "I saw beaver and mink tracks and deer trails. My father taught me to hear."

John Dark Sky took us up Esopus Creek to Black Creek in late April and when we came to the waterfall, he stopped to ask what we saw.

"I see the dark water; then it spins down to the rapids and is white."

"I don't see anything," Moses said. "It looks black running under the bank here."

John Dark Sky was looking away from the dark water. He asked, "What is in the water?"

There was a clear blue sky and the blueberry bush was white in blossom but the water was dark. Black from under the falls to the far bank. Dark and moving. Moving under the bank. Fish. A thousand fish. More. Moving, roiling, blocking the white foam. Moses saw them then. We had not seen them on the way up Esopus Creek. But here at the falls.

"How do the fish come to be here?" I asked John Dark Sky.

"Fish come from the ocean," he said.

Tens of thousands of fish moving as if herded across a vast expanse of land through storms and up along the river and over locks to get to the place where dark water runs under the banks.

"Fish come back home," John Dark Sky added. "They leave the next month."

"They spawn," Moses said.

We came back the next month. "What do you hear?" John Dark Sky asked before we came to the rapids.

"Besides the sound of the water?" I asked.

"Good. The water is all."

The fish had gone. White foam was running down through the rapids.

Farther up Black Creek, above the falls, we found a deer run with more tracks printed in the moss. "What is that smell?" John Dark Sky asked.

I did smell the rank, damp skunk cabbage in the marsh, the faint perfume of blueberries, the wet oily smell of John Dark Sky's moccasins. But that was not what he meant.

"I don't make out anything," Moses said.

John Dark Sky looked over at the bush on the riverbank.

"Yes, the bush," I said; then I saw the branches of the bush move. A twelve- or fourteen-point buck went back to his grazing. Birds flew up as a breeze puffed along the creek. Then the buck was gone.

"If you keep telling us, we might not learn the signs near as well as you," I said.

But he knew we would find them to the west.

His father had not needed to show John Dark Sky the signs. John Dark Sky had already learned them. He found he was supposed to offer maize meal at the mouth of the dead deer and ask forgiveness and praise the Father of the Hunt and pray for a successful hunt the next hunt. But his father had not ordered these rites. He had known them from hearing the old stories.

I had to be shown because I could not listen to the old stories. One hundred years before, John Dark Sky's people had left the Hudson River, "travelled the way we will," he said. But he had come back to the old lands.

"And what about the painter?" Moses asked, interrupting me.

"The panther too. Because it had killed sheep and one dog when I was seven. Shep's father was a pup and the panther threw him off."

"I don't see nary a hole in the hide," Moses said. "Where did the knife enter?"

There, in the back, he slices the panther's backbone in half, John Dark Sky taking the panther's charge and breaking inside the slashing paws and making his cut at the base of the skull from behind. The panther drops, paralyzed.

"But not the throat? Behind the head?"

"The panther was already on him."

"Or he may have wanted to start the skinning at that point," Moses observed.

"He may have. Except his father could not have taught him that."

"No. That is now your old story."

II

Uncle Peter held the rope loosely in his one hand. He made an extra loop around the singletree in case the mules moved too fast for the sheep. The wagon had been ready since sunup, covered with a tarp to keep dust and flies off the barrel of apples and the sacks of dried beans and rice that Cotton packed, the jerky, corn meal, and two jugs each of molasses and whiskey both Cotton and Uncle Peter wanted, the tobacco and box of shells and Remington rifle Uncle Peter didn't shoot anymore but wanted to take it to give an air of authority to the trip: "Else why would two men and 150 sheep and four mules and a horse be working across the country? Unless they had a gun to at least show they were settlers, not just farmers on a Sunday outing."

"You still intend to work the sheep on Sundays?" Father asked.

Uncle Peter looked at Father. "I intend to help you carry out your pledge to Lieutenant Harrison and his wife."

"We shall start along in another three weeks. Are you certain you and Cotton have the way in mind?"

"No certain needed, John," Cotton said. "These maps John Dark Sky made follow the barge canal and the rivers."

"Yes," Father said, "but it does not show where to stop and rest the sheep and yourselves."

"The sheep are restless. They'll thrive as they move." Uncle Peter tapped his hat down lower on his forehead.

"And where will you and Cotton rest?" Father asked, ignoring Uncle Peter's assessment of the sheep.

"Wherever the Hudson and the Mohawk and the other rivers and creeks join. That's where the grasses will be lush. We'll rest there."

John Dark Sky looked out across the Hudson River.

"Well. We will be along. Three weeks or so."

"I'll tell the Harrisons you are coming," Uncle Peter said.

"Tell them I'll be back if I have already arrived in Boscobel and I miss you on the way back to find you," Father said and smiled.

Uncle Peter snapped the reins and the mules and wagon left our road and joined the dust on the Albany Post Road. On a horse Father had given him, Cotton followed, with 150 sheep and three dogs.

"Their first stop, Roundout Creek," Moses said. "That's where the rivers join."

"Yes, but the grass is dry there too," I said, looking down the road as the wavy lines of dust rose. Then they were gone.

Moses and I sat on the porch after we helped Cotton's wife Sarah with the wood. Their baby chewed the beanbag Sarah made. "Poor little Ruth," Moses said. "You shall have to travel a long ways to see your daddy."

John Dark Sky came around the stable from our road.

"Your father wants to see you," he said. "Over at the gate."

III

"Jesse, do you think Peter and Cotton will be able to get there?" Father asked. He was replacing a brace for the crossbar on the gatepost.

I stumbled over my reply. "I think Uncle Peter can make it, only not alone. But Cotton can get them both there."

"Good. I believe the sheep will be all right, but I worry Cotton will feel obliged to keep going when both he and Peter should rest. We may have to travel some Sundays ourselves." He gave me the hammer and used both arms to lift the crossbar back into its bracket.

All morning the shreds of clouds gathered. Clouds, thunderheads, scud under the lowering sky. Thunderheads were rolling up in the east by noon. Then there was no breeze rippling the current in the river, nothing but the loud rasp of cicadas in the stifling July air. The sky became yellow and a few gulls flew overhead. Going to try freshwater clams for a change perhaps.

Our sheep were feeding in the paddock where each day Moses and I spread the marsh grasses we cut. The railroad frightened the sheep more and more and scattered them farther than Shep and the other dogs could fetch.

"Better bring the sheep into the barn," Father said, looking east. He gathered the rope, the post hole digger, the adz and a few rasps and walked towards the house.

Moses, with Shep, was already working the sheep into the barn when I got there. He looked over at the house where Sarah was lashing two shutters together. "Mother closed most of the windows in the house," he said. "She says a big storm is coming."

A sudden, hot, swirling gust lifted his hat and blew it into the barn. Dust, hay and leaves swept through the open barn door as the sheep clattered into stalls.

Father appeared with a rope. "Fetch…" but his words flew by. He called something into the barn and Moses and Shep came out. The lambs started to come back out but Father waved them back in and closed the door, all but the one-half foot he wedged open with his hammer. He wound the rope around the catch and across to the jamb and back again.

"Here….the train back early…" Moses called but he was shouting into the wind so I could not hear the rest of what he said.

The train was taking a long time passing. But then it could not be the train because the wind would be blowing its sound away too fast. Father pointed to the house and ran towards his horse. Why had he not put Boca in the barn with the sheep?

I saw the river flowing upward into the yellow sky over my shoulder as Moses and I made for the porch on a dead run. My ears were popping, the same as I had felt when John Dark Sky took us two days to the Shawangunk Ridge to see west where we were going. And now we weren't sweating. My ears were popping again and I didn't see John Dark Sky.

Shep scurried through the opening that Father still hadn't closed in the storm doors. Moses, then I, followed. A growling roar followed us into the cellar.

"Where did John Dark Sky go?" I asked when the terrific noise stopped and my ears were done popping. "And where is Boca?"

"John Dark Sky has taken Boca and has gone to Peter and Cotton to bring them back," Father said, "but only if there is something to bring."

"Is this a tornado?" I asked.

"It was. It is past now."

A tornado. I wanted to go outside to see it again except the rain was gushing too hard to see anything. A tree was across the storm door and Father could not close the door. He hooked his macintosh to the tree and the door hinge to keep most of the rain out. Rain was coming in around the flapping coattails and under the top step and down the stairs.

Sarah's baby had not cried out during the storm, or maybe I hadn't heard her cries, but she was squalling now.

Father unhooked his allagash and wrapped Sarah and Ruthie in it.

When the storm was over, we went outside under a bright sun. The sky to the west was blue but still dark north over the river. Gullies of claywater were rushing past our chicken coop and runoff from the pasture churned down to the river.

Moses stood in a wash where the stairs going down into our chicken coop bungalow had been. "It hurts my legs it's going so fast," he laughed. "Let's go see how the lambs are doing."

The limb that had come down across the storm door and across the porch was too big to pull off with the mules. Father was chopping at the branches with his axe. Smaller pine and trash littered the road. Moses and I cleared those over behind the hedgerow next to the Post Road. The roadpath was gullied down past the gate Father had been working on before the tornado.

Sarah was singing to her child. The little girl was quiet now.

"Get the sheep back out, while you are here," Father said between axe strokes. "And turn the hay and spread it out to dry. The others will be back, soon," he added.

"With John Dark Sky."

"What will there be to bring back?" Moses wondered as he forked the salt hay.

"If John Dark Sky finds them," I said.

"It won't be the road they have to fight back along," Moses said.

The next day after the storm the wagon, relieved of its cargo and tipping on one skid where a back wheel had been, limped back with the mules roped to the axle. Uncle Peter sat next to Cotton on the driver's seat. John Dark Sky, on Boca, was leading Cotton's horse.

Fewer than twenty sheep were with them, mostly the lambs.

"The wagon lifted right up off the road and set back down going the other way. But the wheel broke off. It was luck that we had unhitched the mules," Cotton explained as we sat on the porch. "The sheep went off every way you can imagine. The dogs got them mostly back to the road, but those sheep won't go near to the river. Not for a while. I suspect."

Uncle Peter's wagon had been set down hard and the tarp and bags of supplies, even the apples in the barrels, had been thrown out over the road and washed away.

"You held onto that rifle right well, Peter," Cotton said, as we watched Uncle Peter clean and oil the metal blue again.

It was not a complete loss. Father even thought it was a blessing. The sheep, all but the lambs and a few ewes, were pastured at a neighbor's, a Quaker farmer north of Kingston, and Cotton had already fitted a new ash axle onto a spare wheel. Sarah was stitching Uncle Peter a tarp we had planned to use. We could fashion a schooner top for our wagon. Better anyway, I thought.

Uncle Peter had lost time, mostly, and was ready to be persuaded to stay until we could all go together. "John, that wind showed me the need for togetherness. I'da been all right with the two wagons side by side."

Only this time it was Father who favored two drives. "If we had been with you, we both could have lost everything. Going two separate times, we take only half the risk." And as usual, Father's rule was adopted. There were to be two drives, and ours would commence in September.

Uncle Peter's sheep were to be gathered from the Baxters' farm after he passed again through Kingston. Uncle Peter and Cotton would take the newly packed barrels of apples, his twenty lambs and twenty more of our bigger lambs ("Maybe now the lambs will be less skittish," Father said), new sacks of beans, cornmeal, rice and another jug each of molasses and Cotton's whiskey. He took his Remington rifle and another box of bullets, his tobacco and the same three good dogs. This time he also took the hides John Dark Sky had found blown across the road off the side of the barn. Three barrels of whale oil had been carried up the river currents from Poughkeepsie and washed up on what used to be Uncle Peter's riverfront. He took one and left Sarah the other two.

Father and Cotton rebuilt the part of the porch damaged in the storm. Father admired Cotton's axle repair. But Father almost looked relieved to see Uncle Peter's wagon leaving once again.

"It won't be a month of Sundays," Uncle Peter told him, looking down from the wagon seat. "More likely only a dozen now."

"That many?" Father asked, smiling again. "Not two?"

"Two dozen, likely," Uncle Peter said.

"Two Sundays; Christmas, yes, and maybe Easter."

"Maybe," Uncle Peter said.

For days after the storm, Sarah had labored to save what crops could be saved, replanting the corn before the sun scorched it, gathering windfall pears, and apples even though they were not yet full ripe. Our smaller fields had not yet burned out like our neighbors', and through the rows of corn uprooted by the sheets of water that stripped the once again scorched soil, Sarah had taken Ruthie out with her, on a blanket next to her, to rescue, stalk by stalk, those remaining stalks. Stunted stalks, but at least she rescued dwarfed ears of corn shrunken inside occasional husks, row after row. While Father and we cleared downed limbs, Sarah patiently scooped the earth back over roots, straightened the bent corn, and staked it with cut up branches of the rock maples Father had hastily stripped, and she carried Ruth daily through the little rows she irrigated with runoff from the ice house.

John Dark Sky watched as she carefully mulched between the plants with ragged maple leaves and seed clusters. "Good. Not pine needles, leaves," he said. With Cotton, he had planted the dry fields in April, placing in the furrows remains of the herring Sarah had not pickled, and the oak bark he had used to tan skins.

Father and Uncle Peter had doubted her judgment. "I have no faith there will be any corn much less anything except standing kindling," said Father. He watched as Sarah troughed the runoff from the ice house and directed the trickles along a trench down through the rows. He watched the soil turn darker, then cake on top and harden.

In the two weeks after Uncle Peter departed, her saved rows of corn had grown only a little higher, but they had not withered as had all the fields on both sides of the river.

The grasses down to the rails were again the color of Father's hair, but Moses and I kicked at the clods near the ends of Sarah's rows and found earthworms underneath, not in powder, but in clayey cakes that clung to roots, and under them, cooler earth that felt almost damp.

"Because the rows are planted pointed downhill." Moses figured it out.

"But if it rains, everything will wash away," I said.

"If it rains," Moses said.

"You may not have anything left in the ice house by September," Father said to Sarah, "but at least you'll have husks to separate the blocks for next January's ice."

And he brought bushels of sawdust too for the ice.

Sarah was darker-skinned than the damp earth. Cotton was no darker than John Dark Sky. Ruthie, their daughter, was in-between, the shade of tanning water.

"Then how did you skin become so dark?" I asked Moses as we lay in our coop, listening to the crickets and peepers.

"Your color is not so light," Moses said.

"But you are darker even for Negro blood."

"I remember my father's skin," Moses said. "He said it was like the mahogany that grew in Martinique."

"But that is red-brown. John Dark Sky's is that color," I said, thinking of my mother's mahogany bureau and mirror.

"Where it grows my father said the mahogany forests are tall and dark and no light penetrates the leaves."

I could not see Moses even though he was there on the cot next to mine. The crickets chattered near us, just outside our coop walls.

"Did you love him?" I asked.

"Not love. You love your father. I was afraid he might kill your father."

"But Father found buyers for his refinery sugar, bought it himself for the Union army."

"I don't know why then," Moses said. "Maybe because your father also gave land back to the Southerners. To abuse."

"Ah," I said. "They would not work the soil, only take from it."

"I can only guess that's why," Moses said.

"Unless it was your mother," I said, a long time later.

"Your father needed her then," Moses said. "And he needed Cotton."

"And Cotton and Sarah needed each other," I offered.

"And they needed your father," he said.

And we went to sleep: one, dark-skinned; one, white skinned, in our coop. Would it be the last week we would share it? Would Moses move in with his mother and Cotton when we returned? Would we return?

IV

I OFTEN WONDERED WHETHER Father loved Sarah, or merely admired her. It was clear she respected him, but not clear what her feelings about him were. They neither one talked about the garrison in New Orleans, or only talked about those things to Cotton. Cotton reminisced openly about the garrison and Father's manipulation of the traders. But not about anything else that happened there in Louisiana.

Moses and I had been friends from the first minute he arrived in Esopus. He was up on the front of the rig on John Dark Sky's return from the train. Sarah and Cotton rode in the back. Uncle Peter lay in the back with them.

Moses and I moved into the abandoned chicken coop overlooking the then green pasture where the sheep grazed. We fashioned a better ceiling by using the broad floorboards. We dug a foundation under the existing floor. Then we hewed boards from the trunk of cedars the railroad had cut down on land that had belonged to Uncle Peter. We dug dirt stairs into the side of the hill down the road.

Moses was 13 and taller than I was. I was a year beyond him in Friends School in Poughkeepsie. The Quakers enrolled Moses when Father wrote to Headmaster Hurd that Moses could write in French as well as in English. Sarah spoke French to Moses. It had been his grandfather's language too, a borrowed language imposed on the Martiniquees by French plantation owners.

We lay on blankets on pallets in the chicken coop on the cedar floor that had come from Uncle Peter's trees and listened to the night sounds. Moses said, "Mother told me

Your grandfather came to New Orleans to start the sugar refineries and he raised your father to adulthood before going back. Your father remained to manage the biggest refinery on his own island, deeded to his father by the King's grant, part of the large island below Natchez. When New Orleans fell, your father gave harbor to hundreds of refugee slaves terrified by advancing Union soldiers.

"Later, Mother told me

I came down too to the island with several score more. Your father held us all like a fief.

Moses talked on in the manner that I understood was Cotton's story.

"Sarah was brought into the main house. She bore Moses and they were settled in the large house built by a black, King's charter landholder.

"The Union Army burned the sugar crops all across Louisiana, effectively cut off the livelihood of many, including the free, black man who became a tenant on his own land. The hundred black slaves he sheltered returned to the plantations of their former masters or worked their way up the Mississippi River. I, Cotton, and his son, stayed.

"I signed on as a field cook with your father's regiment. The regiment had garrisoned what was left of Fort Jackson and Fort St. Philip in New Orleans.

"Colonial Stiles brought Sarah and Moses to the fort to interpret the French of the Cajun trappers and ships' captains. Your father, Colonial Stiles, conducted business at the garrison after the Union Navy steamed in and took over the port without a fight."

Moses continued the story. "Only the Cajuns," Moses said, sleepily, in between the scrabbling sounds in our coop walls, "and a few freed slaves worked the docks. Still, Jesse, your father kept the river trade open. Fur trappers came down from St. Louis, those that slipped by or bribed the troops at Vicksburg. Shrimpers unloaded their nets. Packet boats came with sugar cane from Hispanola and Cuba.

"Your father sent his Union troops with the sugar cane to the island in the Mississippi River and brought back molasses. Your father's troops brought cotton to the port and had it baled. He had the bales and molasses loaded onto ships. And afterwards, when the long lines of slaves returned, marching back to New Orleans from I reckon Georgia, through Mississippi, from Alabama, from probably Tennessee too, where the Union Army told them to go back, that they were free to go back, your Father put these former slaves into the fields to pick the cotton and cut the sugar cane that had not been destroyed and put these men and women on the docks beside the Cajuns working the docks and put them even onto ships going back to Cuba and Hispanola and paid them freed men's wages with the profit from the sale of Louisiana sugar.

"And with those wages, some of the former slaves, a few began to buy the land the carpetbaggers were selling back at cost or almost cost. Your father waited before sending the carpetbaggers packing, waited to buy the land only for what the carpetbagger had paid because the garrison was commissioned even after the Battle of New Orleans, for almost a year after the Battle, and he convinced the carpetbaggers that conscription was within his immediate powers.

"And then when the defeated Southern officers began to return, your father gave them back their land with some of the same Negro men to work it that they had owned but by then barely recognized, some of their men now working that land already and beginning to force it to produce more, working it side by side with that tortured Confederate Army until it healed."

Moses, by then eleven he told, served as Cotton's assistant cook. Some of the things he did impressed Father, and Father offered to send Moses to Esopus to live. Sarah insisted that she go too, and Cotton came too because Father's regiment had nearly completed its tour. As it turned out, Uncle Peter needed attending to, and so Father went north with them all, Moses and Sarah and Cotton. And Uncle Peter.

Neither Cotton nor Sarah discussed their lives on the island. Moses had to piece it together for me. Father was never there, but Union troops were. Moses remembered their coming across the wide space of river in borrowed rowboats, poling from the shore upstream and rowing into the current to arrive at the mangroved tip of the island and then poling into the channels Moses' father and his men dug into the interior.

Moses remembered seeing the Union Navy's ships from the windmill next to the three-story house his father had built.

"Blades pumped water into a large elevated tank inside the windmill where I would spend long idle hours on hot summer days."

Water ran from the tank to the main house and the refinery. Cotton always knew where to find Moses to send him off with important messages for the refinery crews. And the Union Army had put the sugar refinery temporarily out of business by burning the sugar cane across Louisiana before they came to the island. After they arrived, Moses ran errands for a Lieutenant Harrison, Father's Charge d'Affairs on the island, until Lieutenant Harrison lost his leg.

"I ran all the way from the windmill to the boat where Union troops had carried Lieutenant Harrison after two of my father's men shot him." Moses was whispering more quietly than the crickets. "I told the sergeant how to navigate the channels and how to enter the main current to get away from the island and down to New Orleans."

Lieutenant Harrison lived, although his leg was too badly shattered to be saved. Reports of Moses came with the platoon that brought in the wounded lieutenant. Union troops returned to the island in force, only to find that Moses' father had already hanged the insurgents and taken residence in the house again. Father sent for Moses.

"When Colonial Stiles called for me, my father allowed me to go to New Orleans. Later," Moses remembered, "when Mother was needed to take care of me, my father allowed her to leave, and Cotton to accompany her to cook for the Union troops, as payment for not prosecuting."

Sarah probably had known that Moses was not severely ill. Consumption, no; more probably whooping cough or croup, but the message, hand written on U.S. Army stationery and delivered by the sergeant who knew the channels, alarmed Sarah enough to warrant her going: "…indicate an illness of sufficient gravity not to remove the boy…".

Cotton and Sarah packed a small valise and left with the sergeant. Sarah remained as Father's interpreter, and Cotton. "To repay my father for his loss of their services," Moses figured, "your father sent a boat to deliver sugar cane that was beginning to come in and to help transport molasses back to the garrison."

Moses recovered fully and left, with his mother and Cotton and with Father, to take Uncle Peter to Washington. He did not see his birth father again. Sarah was quite sure he would never send for her when he sold his refinery. But Cotton wanted to wait. And then, after one half-year in Washington and the rest of their year together in Esopus, he must have figured she had been right.

V

SHEP WAS AWARE that something very different was happening, a clear day and no sheep to worry to the riverbank. Only a pen, containing all 150 sheep. A canvas-covered wagon was packed with winter storage apples and potatoes, flour and sourdough, sugar, cornmeal and venison jerky, a maul and two axes, hatchets, a kettle, fishing hooks and a line, a flint and tinder box, soap, Father's razor and whetstone. Father's rifle. Not John Dark Sky's bow and quiver of arrows, but he slipped his rifle into the sling on his saddle. Father packed two blankets, a rope and a crowbar, a two-man saw and a one-man saw. Two Macintosh coats, a Barlow knife, a bag of salt, and a barrel of whiskey, carefully examined for breaks in the seams, each item assigned its place among the cargo in the wagon.

John Dark Sky needed but little: a blanket, a leather pouch, a knife, and a few small boxes that might have contained candles. And he packed his deerskin hides.

Then our orders to bring the sheep with the other dogs, and send the sheep down the road, down to the bridge at Port Ewen with the wagon coming along behind and the sheep in front fanning out to sever what weeds they could along the dusty roadside and hedgerows.

We left Sarah in the yard with Ruth, waving goodbye. The wood Moses and I had stacked up higher than ourselves, Moses having lifted the topmost logs, finally blocked them from view. The rooftop dropped behind a hill as we slowly followed 150 sheep along the Post Road. Shep and two other dogs would have a busy time of it. They would have to follow them the livelong day and nip the stray lambs back to the flock. The ewes wouldn't go after them, for they seldom remembered their lambs.

Moses and I took turns sitting on the wagon next to Father and riding on his fine horse, Boca. John Dark Sky rode beside. Father kept the mules moving, along the wider stretches in shade, then, where the road narrowed, across the bridge over Roundout Creek, then on the shady side again where the road widened as we came into Kingston. Kingston. Where we would come to buy sacks of flour, clothes for school and where we went to Quaker Meeting.

"Mighty glad to be buying nothing at the emporium," Moses said. We would not need new clothes or shoes for school this year. Father said the journey's experience was going to be just as important for us, and I reckon from the way we were enjoying life so far, it would be.

"Nor selling the sheep," I said. It always bothered me a little to take sheep to market. But we had to have supplies and supplies called for trade or cash, which were the same things as far as Father was concerned. I didn't understand greenbacks and neither did Moses. To Moses, it was all as useless as Confederate script, but I guess we had an obligation to figure it all out. Just not this year. This year it would have to be sheep as script.

We didn't even stop in Kingston. I guess it would have been unseemly for 150 sheep to graze on the town green. The flowers some of the townspeople planted and watered weren't for the sheep to devour. We went right on through, out of town, past the road to Woodstock, and on through Lake Katrine. The riverbank sloped more gradually now, and we kept to the river road where it was somewhat cool and grassy for the sheep.

Baxters' farm was the first place we would stop. Father wanted to pay his respects to the family who had been so kind to Uncle Peter in the storm. And to refill our water jugs. The river would do for the sheep and mules, but Father said until we were a stretch more above Kingston, we had better find well water. The tide brought Kingston's sewerage upstream almost to Hudson he had heard. John Dark Sky said he had heard that the water was once fit to drink all the way down to Poughkeepsie.

The Baxters' daughter Susan was in our classes at Friends' school, and Moses fancied her. I thought she was about as forward as any girl I knew and told Moses to make a fool of himself if he wanted to. Sure enough, there she was looking at the sheep as we herded them past the Baxters' gate.

"I'd go with you in a minute if daddy would let me," she said as we took our tea apart from the adults. "Now you just sit down and then I'll hand you your cups," she ordered. She put her hand on Moses' arm. I took the cup she handed me and went over and sat on the millstone steps nearer the adults. Susan was clattering away at Moses like a train and he was nodding and gesticulating back. It made me want to gag.

Here we were on the most peaceful and important experience American men could have, and Moses was acting like he would have preferred dancing. I looked away. John Dark Sky looked the other way too, I noticed, his head toward the river.

I was glad to be sitting near him, to take after his silence and his sense of purpose, to try to gain his strength and his wisdom. He seemed to know not just how to plan for whatever would come next but to know what it would be.

I looked upriver with him and tried to see what it was he saw. But all I could see was river, narrower here than it was at Esopus, and lines of hills off in the west. North, the way we were heading was an endless ribbon of water disappearing into the trees.

VI

As I placed my teacup on the tray, the next-to-worst thing that could have happened was taking place. Father was entertaining the idea of staying for supper at the Baxters. Then, the worst thing that could possibly happen began to happen.

"And please rest the night with us, John." Goody Baxter was saying.

Please, good father of mine, don't let it happen.

"We couldn't impose, Elizabeth," Father began. "It's already been so much you've done for us and for Peter."

"Fiddlesticks!" she said. "You'll just bed those boys down right here on the porch and yourself and John in the parlor on our davenport and daybed. I've linens for all."

"Moses, Jesse, what do you say? We do honor the Lord tomorrow and likely will not make Saugerties regardless if we leave tonight. The Baxters' hospitality will be our blessing for a good drive ahead."

Moses was nodding like a partridge cock in mating season. I knew it was beyond hope. Now we'd be here all night and the next day too. It just was the worst luck.

Susan Baxter came up all smiles and took us both by the hand and ran us down the porch steps. "Oh, come, yippee! Let me show you the fat old woodchuck out in the cow pasture and the pheasant chicks." She was a born flibbertigibbet, a corn tassel in a gale. I was so downright put out I could have cried. And there was Moses pulling me on a crack-the-whip and I was sent sprawling down the hill to the pasture. It wasn't fun anymore. This was the hard work part Father must have meant.

We came in from woodchucks and pheasant chicks and rope-the-heifers and washed up at the well for supper. Goody Baxter had fried up cornmeal mush that smelled for all the world like the good one Cotton makes, and a roast was on the sideboard, carved into slabs a half-inch through. It perked up my spirits to see the gravy boat steaming on the table and the crabapple jelly and a blueberry pie come out with Susan.

She had put a ribbon in her braid that I pretended not to notice, but Moses looked over at me and winked as she tossed her braid and turned back toward the kitchen, so I knew he liked it.

Goody Baxter came in wiping her hands on her apron and sat closest to the kitchen door on the bench. Susan backed through the swinging door carrying a water pitcher and a salad bowl. Tomatoes. All was lost and gone. We would have to taste some to be polite.

And then, after our silent Quaker grace, I saw Moses help himself to two slices of tomatoes and pass the bowl to Father who took some and passed it on.

There was never a bigger farce than to see Moses smack his lips as he slid a slice into his mouth and roll his eyes towards the ceiling and exclaim, "My, oh my, I never had a better tomato, Goody Baxter!"

I had to do it and I'm sorrier for it than I ever have been. It was like stepping on a slug, but I did it and I ate that tomato slice in a gulp and grabbed for a biscuit.

Susan looked over and smiled.

I admit the biscuits beat Cotton's and the roast was plenty good. I was just hoping the memory of the tomato would fade when the time came for the blueberry pie.

After the main course, John Dark Sky thanked the Baxters and left the table to see to the sheep. Less than a minute later, Moses did the foolhardiest stunt I ever saw in all my born days. He edged his plate towards the center of the table and said, "I declare, Goody Baxter, I'm unable to take another bite. Much as that blueberry pie tempts me, better discretion tells me to restrain. I'll ask to be excused and help John Dark Sky bed the sheep down before it's night."

When had he ever restrained from anything except tomatoes? And what was this game? He was excused and he took his plate out through the kitchen door.

He could be a dolt. I'd be happy to have his portion, and he could hope I wouldn't laugh him off the porch later.

Then, all of a sudden I knew what was up. He was seeing if Susan would get out of the dishes and come out with him. But was he ever going to be fit to be tied! She just kept sitting looking like a Sunday school girl, smiling at me. I couldn't stand it.

So when Goody Baxter got around to me for pie, I said, "I do believe I'm overwhelmed like Moses, ma'am. I thank you, but I'm too full to fit another bite in." I meant it when I added, "It was delicious." Everything except the tomatoes.

"Would you like to join Moses and John Dark Sky then?" Goody Baxter asked.

"Yes, ma'am, if I may," I said and looked away from the blueberry pie.

I went out through the kitchen with my empty plate and tore out after Moses to give him a piece of my mind. Leaving blueberry pie to be heroic or polite or I don't know what.

The Quaker meeting house was a stone, one-room building with a slate roof next to the old capitol building in Kingston. The cool feeling of the room and the sunlight streaming through the window onto the facing benches helped the spirit that was supposed to pass between the 32 other Friends. Try as we might, even at the Wednesday morning school meetings, neither Moses nor I ever could feel that spirit. But I could tell it was there because it was the only time Susan sat still for such a long spell. And at school the others, like her, would keep still for almost an hour each Wednesday at meeting. I didn't see why girls needed to be on the other side of the Meeting house if they weren't going to be flirtatious, and Moses wanted like anything to have them all around him so he could breathe them in or hear them breathing. He told me so. But most of the elders wanted to keep separate seating. Moses was too new to the school to get involved in the debate, and I don't know where Father stood on the issue, but it wouldn't have made any difference. Those elders were set in their ways.

As we walked through Kingston market after Meeting, we saw squashes and potatoes, berries and four different kinds of pickled herring, pots, pans, sheep and oxen that farmers' families brought into town every

Sunday morning spring, summer and fall. Families from West Park and Saugerties, and some down from Woodstock, and our neighbors from Esopus and Port Ewen gathered after worshipping and traded goods with others at the market. The few farmers who had any corn were soon bought out. Seed corn was needed even if there would be no maize for cornmeal this dry fall.

Moses and I had ridden in with the Baxters on their wagon and Father came later, just before Meeting, on John Dark Sky's horse. John Dark Sky stayed at the Baxters' farm to finish shoeing Boca and to tend the sheep.

Susan fluttered back and forth from wagon to wagon, looking at the goods and talking to everyone and admiring the oxen like some country fair judge. I was getting a whopping yearning to light out for the Baxters, all seven miles, but just as I was about to tell father I was going to walk back, Goody Baxter came over to Moses and me with a basket.

"We're going to have some vittles now, so join us over behind the Meeting house. You boys may have worried that your pieces of pie were squandered, but you needn't have feared. Susan said you'd want them, so she bundled them up in the picnic basket."

That placated me, all right. And so did the picnic – cold jugs of milk, boiled eggs, some of last night's biscuits, and smoked sausages and cheese all the way across the river from the smokehouse in Pine Plains. Father bought some at the market for our trip and as a present for the Baxters.

We lay around after dinner talking about the storm and how dry it was even afterwards and about how the railroad might be used to carry livestock to the big markets in New York and even Boston. The Baxters were stockholders in the railroad. They pointed out how a trip like ours would take a mere two weeks or less to Chicago.

"Would the train run on the Sabbath?" asked Father.

John Dark Sky was standing next to Father's newly shoed horse, beside the Baxters' gate, combing the burrs out of Shep's coat. He looked up as we wandered into the lane, although he probably knew we were coming. Father stopped to talk to John Dark Sky, then looked out over our flock of sheep, grazing peacefully with the Baxters' cattle along the edge of the road. The cattle had already cropt the roadside grass, but our sheep were reducing it more so. At super, potato pancakes and applesauce, Father talked of the drought. "John Dark Sky says, and I agree, that the sheep are going to need shelter middays. It's almost too much for us. This heat worries the sheep into whatever cover they can find – a ditch, a log. They even scuffed out a little hollow in your pasture today and crawled in to get out of the sun. We'll have to quit before noon and travel evenings then."

"Not this evening, surely," Fred Baxter said.

"Well, Fred, it looks to be clear," Father said. "We might try to stay closer to Peter."

"Been a couple of weeks now, I believe," Fred said. "I reckon he'll be along about Utica if not farther. How are you going?"

"We'll stay along the water where we can," Father said. "On the barge canal most of the way after the Mohawk drops off."

"The railroad's through there too." Fred said. "And it's a pretty rough gang on that canal. I'd stick to the railroad."

"Maybe, but we'd like to be nearer the water." Father pushed his plate aside and drew an imaginary map on the table. "The railroad and the river, yes, until Schenectady. Then the river to the canal, I'd say. For the Sheep."

We picked up our plates and silverware and went through the kitchen outside to hitch the mules to the wagon. John Dark Sky already had them in their traces. Moses and I helped work the sheep out to the gate.

Susan hung on the gate as we persuaded the last of the sheep out onto the road. The sun was setting in back of the Catskills.

"We'll be back in a few days," Moses kidded.

"I'll pick some more blueberries, in that case." She was as silly as always.

Father came up the wagon, and John Dark Sky rode behind on his horse, holding the reins on Father's horse. "You make your way along the river to Saugerties," Father told me. John Dark Sky handed me Boca's reins.

We should have been there last night. Although, it had been civilized at the market. I had to admit.

"Maybe we're not going to take all year after all," I said to them, half convinced.

"Oh, it will be all year anyway," Moses said. "But our friends will still be here when we get back." He glanced over at Susan.

The wagon slowed to let the last of the sheep through. John Dark Sky was last through the gate. Then Susan latched it.

It was peaceful swinging on Boca. He had been a little gimpy since Kingston, but John Dark Sky fixed him up regular, as he would the mules if they became lame. And the moon came up, a waning quarter. It was going to be clear enough breeze to cool us all. Then it was night and I could just make out the sheep ghostlike along the roadside ahead of me. Shep or one of his daughters barked once. The river was quiet. Crickets stopped their sawing songs as we went by, then started singing again after we passed.

VII

I CALLED SHEP AND the other dogs to stop the flock on a rise over the river. Lights on the opposite shore meant we must be nearly to Catskill. We weren't though, as I found out when Father brought the wagon up.

"Not Catskill, Jesse. But you found a good place to camp. This will be fine until dawn. Then we can try for Catskill by noon."

A cluster of shimmering lights on the opposite shore lit up someone's gaudy celebration. We had heard of princely splendor of the storied mansions farther down the river, and I once visited Boscobel House, the older one down to near New York City, with Father, but on the opposite shore across from our camp must have been a palace. I imagined a ball with dancers and pipers all night. As we watched, windows lit with a glow, Moses and I talked about the extravagance. Then the long day caught up to us and we stretched out our blankets on the dry grass and slept.

It wasn't quite light enough to see the river when I awoke, but I saw the sheep all around us curled up with their legs tucked under or standing under a tree near the road, ruminating. The lights on the opposite bank of the river had gone out. Stars had shifted to a point lower in the sky.

When I awoke again, John Dark Sky was poking up the fire and Father was readying some pancakes for us. Moses stirred and I shook him.

"Come on, breakfast, lazy bones."

"Go on. I'll fetch some on the way," he said and rolled over. "Is that ball still going?"

"No. They quit about an hour ago. I went across to dance the last few dances, though," I boasted.

"You must have been dreaming," he said, sitting up and stretching.

"Dreaming, yes," I said.

Father's pancakes were hot, but not light like Cotton's. I was polite and finished mine, but I noticed Father gave the rest to the dogs. The sheep were up and trying to find shoots of grass that weren't there. The whole bank down to the Hudson was dry. I could see the river and the railroad tracks alongside clearly in the sunlight. It was narrower here on the Hudson, not even one-half mile across, and the water was low. Eroded banks were exposed where it must usually have run higher.

We stopped between the river and Catskill just as the sun reached its zenith. The sheep had already been scuffing the hillocks for shelter and any dampness they could find. Even Shep looked wilted, tail down, ears drooping, and tongue hanging out of the side of his mouth. The mules seemed the only ones unaffected by the noontide heat. They moved along in their harnesses with a mindless patience, the kind of steady march that would get us halfway to Albany today if we needed to be.

If we held to a schedule in any way, it was only in Father's mind, and not something he announced. No one seemed anxious to get to a particular destination. Uncle Peter alone had shown a desire to move along apace, and he had been brought up short by the storm.

I don't believe it was the Lord's doing, that storm, which set Uncle Peter back two weeks. I don't accept that kind of God. On the Sabbath, He rested from His creating but the creatures He had made had to get food, find shelter, and keep away from enemies. God might step back to watch how it all was working, but His workers had to keep moving. I figured I was one of His workers. I know I'm going against Father in this, and Sarah. They honor their Creator by resting, like Him. But it's just another way of honoring God to walk across His earth daily.

"We'll put up here for the afternoon," Father said.

Resting now, at noon – now we all agreed with Father on that. Moses and I hightailed it to the river. Where the rails angled up to the town, we walked on the tender hooks then beat a path down the rest of the way to the river for a swim. It was cold, running fast. We no sooner got used to it and plunged on in than we found ourselves swept along like leaves.

I grabbed an overhanging branch and Moses grabbed my legs and swung straight out north of me in the crosscurrent. The branch bent but didn't give. We pulled ourselves up to the tree and dove in from a higher branch a few times.

Then we hiked back along the shore to the place we had left our clothes and sat on them to dry off. It didn't take five minutes and we were dry, but hot, too, as soon as we had our clothes back on.

"This heat probably doesn't bother you, Moses," I said as we walked back up to the sheep. "Louisiana must have been hot like this."

"Not all the time. And it rained some," he replied. "It's cooler at night here at least."

We found the sheep curled up under trees and Father busy with some ledgers. Even out here on the trail. Planted acreage, cost of seed, expense of shipping whiskey, purchase of one horse from U.S. Army, purchase of adz and one-man saw. Income from sale of 29 acres to New York Central Railroad, from sale of three ewes and 14 lambs, from sale of 26 barrels of whiskey, of one dollar from title to improved lot and property to W. Cotton MacHugh, of four dollars from sale of cedar logs to Moyers Sawmill.

If Cotton and John Dark Sky kept ledgers, it was not obvious. Moses said no, they had figures in their heads. Uncle Peter's ledgers dated to 1861, when he joined the U.S. Army. Then they stopped. Father brought them up to date for Uncle Peter upon returning from the war.

Our routines had just been established – the long, slow, sultry shepherding from early in the morning to noon, resting the sheep, swimming, lazing around while Father repaired the harnesses or trued a wheel. John Dark Sky hunted our supper, usually a rabbit or pheasant. One day, he brought three squirrels. Sometimes Moses and I had luck fishing – shad, sunnies, or black crappies. We could catch them easily with a trotline, set while we swam. After we lingered awhile in the river, we pulled in the line usually with a few fish. We used worms for bait, or grubs. Just above Athens, where the river bent around a sandbar and the current was slower, we used crickets and caught a large bass. But Father couldn't make a bass taste good. Not even Cotton could, so we threw it back.

"You should taste his catfish," Moses said about Cotton's fish dishes.

"He cooked up those bullheads we caught," I remembered. A delicate troutlike flavor emerging through Cotton's fried cornmeal batter. "But they're too hard to clean." First, getting the slimy things off the hook without getting barbed, you had to stake them through the head to the ground. Then you had to take a knife, not any old knife but your sharp knife, and slit the skin around the head in a circle. If you could strip that slimy skin off whole, from head to tail, without leaving any, you were lucky. Finally, you could clean the pinkish yellow flesh and fry it. But it took twice the time to clean those bullheads as any other fish. The real trouble was, they'd swallow the worm every time, so you'd kill them getting the hook out anyway. We usually took the extra time to clean them, rather than throw them back for other fish to eat. And Cotton did fry them up so they tasted close to heaven.

"Not like river cats," Moses said with a distant look in his eye.

"Was the Mississippi a much bigger river?" I asked.

"You couldn't tell it was a river," Moses said. "Water seemed to be all around you, everywhere."

"I mean, could you see across it? Was it as wide as the Hudson down by Bear Mountain?" I asked, thinking as far down as I'd been on the Hudson River.

"You could see across most days," Moses said. "It's just that there wasn't much except more river once you got to the other shore."

"I don't understand," I said. "How can a river not have banks?"

"On, there were brambly islands everywhere. You couldn't tell where the river stopped. Sometimes you'd get out on a stretch of shore and find it had more river on the other side. You'd be on an island."

"Like Esopus Island?" I asked.

"Not anything like Esopus Island. Nothing," Moses said.

"Well, what then?" I was puzzled.

But he couldn't tell me. The best he could come up with was an ice floe. "You take the ice we jumped on." Last winter when the river began to break up, I remembered. "When you walked out to Esopus Island on the ice and then when you jumped onto that shelf at the end of Esopus Island and it broke off?"

"Yes." In panic I reached for the stick Moses stretched out to me. Then I pulled back, against the current, close enough to jump onto the more solid ice he stood on. It was a frightening moment.

"It's like that sometimes," he continued. "You think you're fishing from the riverbank and suddenly you see a paddle boat come around behind you. So you weren't on land, you were on an island. Your spot on the riverbank is a chunk of bramble and mangrove and silt and a whole big river is still there before you get to the other side." I still couldn't imagine it. An entire island floating in a wide river, a river wide enough to be a sea.

"As wide as six Hudsons," Moses said. "And running as fast, only you couldn't tell unless you watched the opposite shore awhile."

"Like the sheep," I said. "They drift along without knowing whether they are on shore or not. Just following the river."

"They could be surrounded by a big river for all they know," Moses added.

"We're taking them wherever we want," I said.

We pulled on our clothes and fishing lines, and I pulled the stringer full of fish out of the river. We wandered back up the bank to the shaded grove near the railroad trestle where Father and John Dark Sky sat, smoking and watching the sky.

"A fish stew for supper," Father said with a wreath of smoke hovering about his head.

We cleaned and scaled the fish and placed them in a pot of sheep's milk heating in a kettle over the fire.

That afternoon Father sold two sheep to a farmer in Coxsackie and came back to find the milk simmered down to a stew with potatoes, onions, carrots, and chunks of slab bacon melted into it all. John Dark Sky had done the cooking, and I was ready to let him do it all, the way it smelled, rich and savory.

It was almost night when we finally ate our hurried meal. We mopped up the last of the stew with a fresh loaf of bread Father bought.

Then we were moving again, into the night, past Coxsackie, passing New Baltimore in the early morning after resting only four hours, then waiting again at noon for the heat to stop raising the river up in layers into the air.

New Baltimore to Albany, a long, two-day ride with one day folding into the next like rivers joining.

VIII

A FEW WAGONS PASSED us going north. And we passed news with other wagons that were heading south. The farmers whose land we crossed almost always asked us about the drought and invited us to pull our wagon into a field or into their barn overnight. Those that had sheep found the same things happening on hotter days – their sheep stayed under trees during the day. One man thought the sheep grazed in the evening to get the moisture. Many farmers kept their sheep along the river's edge, in the weeds and grasses growing there.

Reports of Uncle Peter and Cotton passing through included one farmer who told us that Uncle Peter and Cotton has used his orchard to hold up during the hottest day. That must have been the same, two days before we left home, I recollected. Moses and I had taken the sheep down past the railroad tracks and into the shallow water to cool them.

We ventured into Albany on Tuesday evening of our third week. The sheep, with John Dark Sky, went right through the main part of town, staying along the harbor. Father, Moses and I stopped at the capitol, a tall building on a steep hill. Father said it was like the buildings in Washington. Albany is a busy town, directly on the river. All the townspeople seemed in a tremendous hurry. The carriages went fast, the people walked and talked fast. The trolley made a clatter as it rumble down the street, full of people who could hardly wait to get where they were going. I would have enjoyed that trolley ride and wouldn't have cared where it went or how long it took, but I would not have enjoyed how crowded it was.

We sold three more sheep including the ram I raised from a little black lamb. But Father said the price was more favorable, so I allowed as how it meant he'd be used for wool, not slaughter. That eased my mind somewhat.

The market where we sold the sheep was ten times the size of Kingston's or any I had seen before. All the farmers and fishermen and artisans had their wares out on display along the harbor. The ships that were unloading and loading at the docks looked even bigger at their berths than those I remembered going up the river past our farm.

At the stable where we left Father's horse and the mules for the day, the groom remembered Uncle Peter and Cotton. "Brought four or five sheep in to market so full of brambles and beggars lice you'da thought they was raised in a briar patch," he said. "They was good sheep. Just ragged looking."

Father brought a pair of low shoes at one store, some work gloves and a hat with a wide brim that took the place of the one he had used as a Union officer and still wore. He bought us some fish hooks and line and some stick candy.

He sold two each of John Dark Sky's hides and skins. Father marked it down in a separate ledger.

We walked back to the stable just as the ferry came in to dock. The ferry carried people and carriages, and more people and more carriages were waiting to be ferried to the opposite shore when the unloading was complete. I hadn't ever seen a ferry with a regular schedule like the railroad, but Moses said the ferryboats in New Orleans were bigger still and carried twice as much as the ferry. "Summers, they make five round trips each weekday," he said.

That night we tried a fish called sturgeon. Father bought just the steaks we baked, not the whole fish, which was big as a sheep. I saw it in the market on ice, along with other kinds of fish I had never before seen. The sturgeon was good. I hoped we would find some again.

"Peter must be keeping pretty well ahead, maybe even past Utica," Father said as we rounded up the flock to drive on up the Mohawk River that night.

"Perhaps it's cooler where he is," I said.

"Perhaps," said Father. "It's as far north as we'll be going, I reckon, isn't it, John?" John Dark Sky looked back to see Shep nipping at one lamb.

"Yes," he said as he turned back. "Unless we go to Canada."

"No. I'd be tempted," Father said, "but with Thanksgiving coming on by then, we might have bad weather. We'll stay south of the lakes, and I trust Peter and Cotton will as well."

Albany was behind us then, and I was relieved to see the Hudson free of piers and traffic. We still saw barges and were beginning to see other canal boats – long, narrow ore boats and others filled with coal or trap rock. They were pushed by steamboats through the swift currents flowing northward.

Near the mouth of the Mohawk River grasses were thicker and we came upon more piney trees. The hot, dry air still baked us at noon and we rested in stands of pine. The sheep burrowed right into the needles that piled up on the ground under the tall trees.

We got to the Mohawk River on a cool Sunday morning and camped on a weedy flat shoal outside a small settlement called Cohoes. The first thing I noted about the Mohawk besides that it was smaller than the Hudson was that it was a different color. Maybe it was green because the trees grew closer to the shore, or maybe the reflections of the trees stretched across to the opposite shore. It was not anything like the pewter color we saw all day on the Hudson.

We sat around on the shore and fished the whole day. Our sheep enjoyed a fall day of grazing and only in the hottest part of the day did they come down to the shore. We were stretched out under some willows, waiting for the clothes we washed to dry. Father agreed to let us do the washing even though it was Sunday, since we had such a perfect spot to dry them on the willow branches. The sheep lay in the shade of the overhanging branches, panting. Shep and three other dogs gnawed on stew bones Father tossed to them.

We ate the beef stew that Father stirred over the fire all morning. The dried venison and fresh squirrel and rabbit we had grown used to tasted better, but Father bought the beef in Albany to give us stronger blood for the long trip ahead. I saw there was enough for supper too, so I resigned myself to another meal of it. Moses tolerated it too, but he played with his helping before finishing.

I wondered what kinds of fish we would find in the Mohawk. John Dark Sky told of huge fish called muskellunge and pike and pickerel, other pointed fish with no dorsal fins and sharp teeth, gars. Moses and I talked about those fish, eager to try our luck. But all we caught that afternoon were two small bass, a carp and something John Dark Sky named a red horse, a fish with small sucker mouth like a carp and red fins, but it was a longer, skinnier fish than a carp.

A gray cloud covered the sun and the wind picked up just after supper. The branches of the willows were tossed around. Gusts whipped waves up and down the Mohawk River. Moses and I rescued the clothes before they were tossed into the river and ran to put the supper things into the wagon.

One of the dogs was barking in a thicket. Some sheep had likely wandered in to chew the weeds, and the dog must have been trying to get them back before the storm.

The dog's barking changed pitch and she hied out of the thicket with her hackles up. I started over to help her fetch the sheep. Then she shrieked and jumped, but not in time. A boar's charge lifted her over the scrub brush and into the air, a red gash opening across her back. The boar kept charging through the brush right at me. I froze to the tangle of tree roots under me. The boar dropped its head and its curved tusks pointed at me as chips of tusk splintered. Then the whole tusk disappeared and the boar collapsed in a heap at the base of the tree I was clutching.

Father was shouting something next to me to John Dark Sky. The air smelled like a puffball and my eyes smarted from gunpowder smoke. John Dark Sky bent down, still looking up over the brush, touched the dog, then left her and picked up something. Shep and the other two dogs went through the brush, mouths open, but I did not hear their cries. My hearing was like times when I was under water and Moses would shout.

Father walked past the fallen boar and into the underbrush after the dogs, but turned and came with two things the dogs killed and John Dark Sky came back with two more, their tongues hanging out, right past their mother boar, also dead, and I still could not move away from the tree.

Moses came over and touched my shoulder. Why was he whispering? His mouth opened and closed and I sounded for all the world like his wordless speaking under water.

I shook my head to clear the ringing. "...ran up behind you," Moses was saying, "with his rifle going and missed first, no hit the tusk, then, standing right beside you, killed the boar ten feet in front of you."

Gradually, like distant thunder, my hearing was returning. We walked over to the wagon and I heard Father ask Moses to fetch the salt bucket. Father and John Dark Sky gutted altogether five dead piglets and salted the flesh. The little feet were given to the dogs to gnaw. The dogs seemed oblivious to the absence of one of their number.

The mother boar was gutted and hung from the wagon frame to drain. I could hear fine now. Father's rifle had deafened me for a spell, but my hearing returned. I helped clean and salt the last piglet while Father buried the entrails. We would have pork for the rest month.

"Next time, climb that tree, Jesse," Father said.

"I will. I promise," I replied, and that was all Father said about it.

IX

Any drawing of the Hudson River looking out from our farm in Esopus would have shown a wide, gray band with swirls, trees along the far shore, and a narrow island in the middle. The Mohawk River from Cohoes to Schenectady, a day's drive with the sheep, was a scale of the same swirling water from Esopus to Kingston, but greener. "The Mohawk isn't a river," Moses said. "It's a little green salamander."

The opposite banks of the Mohawk River were wooded like the eastern shoreline of the Hudson. The bracken on the side we were following, the southern side, sloped down to railroad tracks. The tangle of weeds and choke cherry trees and witch hazel along the Mohawk resembled Uncle Peter's riverfront land. Then we found a place where the Mohawk River divided, spanning an island, a long, narrow island with birches and stands of pine. We laughed. A little Esopus Island, a miniature of the place in the middle of the Hudson where Black Creek fed into the river. I took Shep out to Esopus Island to camp on hot days, and I jumped ice floes out to the island winters. I felt at home and forgot about the event of the boar. The sheep stayed away from the brambles, and kept closer to the wagon.

We buried our dog at the source of the Mohawk River. The boar must have broken her back, even if we could have staunched the flow of blood. Her back legs wouldn't move. Father shot her to save her pain. She had been a brave pup, one of Shep's offspring by a neighbor's dog, never afraid of anything.

Our wagon moved along slowly across the level flood plain of the river. Moses pointed out signs of the river's having been much higher – water marks on pilings as we passed a bridge, and tree growth beginning higher up than usual and no houses here on the river.

Moses mentioned other rivers. "It looks like the Hudson but it floods more like the Mississippi, I'd say."

"They must be spring floods," I offered. "Maybe there's more snow up along the river here."

"And more melt off of those mountains," said Moses, looking at the distant hills to the north.

"The Adirondack Mountains lie up a week farther north," Father said from the wagon. "There will be more than enough snow here in four months."

"We'll run into some snow too, won't we?" I asked.

"Yes, we can expect snow in Ohio."

All along the Mohawk River near Schenectady, we found deer runs and otter slides, bear scats full of choke cherry pits, but no more signs of boars, for which we were thankful. As we herded the sheep westward, saplings at the river's edge showed signs of beaver, but their lodges must have been hidden back in the marshes. Muskrats splashed into the banks on one shore, and martins ran along the margin of the near shore. At night, we heard raccoons and smelled an occasional skunk, but none of them approached our campsites, and our dogs kept out of the comings and goings of those creatures.

We moved peacefully along past Schenectady towards Amsterdam. From Amsterdam we followed the Mohawk River towards Fultonville. It was nearing the end of our first month, "an easy month," Father said, even considering the drought and the disturbed sleep hours and the end-of-summer heat we suffered.

Father and I were getting along well since his stern reminder about climbing a tree when the boar charged. Before the war, he was ever after me to be a man, to work harder on my splitting wood, to get more haying done, to fetch up all the milk in one trip instead of two. But the logs he split were just too big for me, and so was the sledge. I preferred the smaller, lighter maul. And the haying got done. And I spilled less milk in two trips, usually. But it was never enough for Father.

I think that he knew his going to war would leave me to fend for myself, and he wanted to prepare me. But he went to war. John Dark Sky stayed. I was fine, and I had grown sturdier. I could feel it.

And Father and I got along quite well after he returned from the war. There had been receptions for him and Uncle Peter and formal ceremonies and hoopla. They brought me along to some and made me feel like a hero too. For one ball, Father dressed in his uniform and looked grand. Uncle Peter did not attend that function, embarrassed still about his hand, I imagine.

Father was invited by a family to several occasions at their summerhouse called Boscobel, a great spread near Croton on the Hudson River. Father took me with him to one. That was the time I saw Bear Mountain, and the river stretched wide, both to the north and west.

Then we spent that entire night at Boscobel. It had been arranged to introduce Father to a young woman from New York whose husband had been killed in the war. She was beautiful, and I think Father was smitten with her. She wore black for her mourning, though, and Father said, as we rode in a passenger rail car home a day later, that she had not recovered from the shock of her husband's death.

I thought she would have made a good wife for Father, although I'm not sure how her two young children would have liked raising sheep.

Father wrote her a few letters and she wrote back, but I guess Father put off pursuing her further. "'Boscobel' reminds me," he said, "and I have that obligation before me first and foremost."

When we reached a level spot on the Mohawk River opposite Fultonville, we were ready for the Sunday rest Father insisted upon. "You are not simply driving sheep; you are driving yourselves." He had said that several times before. Now we knew what he meant. Moses and I ought to sit in the wagon instead of riding Boca. Father's horse was looking tired, and the sheep were growing more cantankerous. To spur them along took more nudging and hollering. One of the dogs fetched up lame and rode with us in the wagon while the other two urged the flock along as well as they could. Only three of them ran the sheep now.

But John Dark Sky looked rested. Mornings, he was always awake and stirring the fire. And he rode erect on his horse and sat straight in the wagon when he took the reins for Father. He may have been showing us the Seneca Indians' endurance, but if so, he never referred to them or to himself as one of them. Whatever it was that shaped him, it made me want to sit straighter and fully finish my turns in the saddle even though my backside ached.

We lazed around the shore opposite Fultonville all Sunday morning, but after our noon meal, Moses and I swam over to Fultonville on the northern side of the river and discovered a statue in the center that town. It was erected in honor of Robert Fulton, who invented the steamboat. Moses said it was the most important invention ever. "It put twice as many boats on the Hudson and the Mississippi," he guessed. "And two iron battleships: one is rusting in New Orleans."

Moses may have been taken with steamers, but I thought the sailing vessels were ever so much better. No smell of smoke, nor fire came from a sailboat, and nowhere near as much trouble was needed to sail as to fire a steamboat. The train, now I admit that was a fine invention, but I preferred the sight of sails on a body of water, even a narrow one such as the Mohawk River, to a smoky, noisy, tornado-like steamboat befouling the waters.

The statue indicated that Robert Fulton named his steamboat after Robert Livingston's house, Clement. Livingston helped Fulton with that first steamboat and Fulton powered it up the Hudson River to Albany, right past those other big Livingston houses we too had passed as we herded the sheep.

"But why did Fulton get a statue of himself here, and a whole town named after him?" Moses asked.

I went around to the other side of the statue where a plaque told of Fulton's inventing the locks used on the Erie Canal. We should go past those in a week or two. The barges pushing east on this stretch of the Mohawk River came from the Eire Canal, and the canal boats being towed up the Mohawk River in our direction were going there.

We came across two boys fishing on the shore in Fultonville. They were interested in our sheep drive and wanted to know about steamboats on the Hudson River.

"You mean you came all the way from near New York to here?" They were amazed. We told them New York because they hadn't heard of Poughkeepsie or Kingston. They had two big suckers and about a dozen crappies strung on a line, and they gave their catch to a friend who had a rowboat. They rowed us across the Mohawk and tied the boat to a falling down dock.

Then we hiked up to where Father and John Dark Sky were smoking. The sheep were milling around in the shade of a huge sycamore. Father had his Union officer's hat over his face. We patted the sheep, while Moses told them about New Orleans and the stern-wheeled paddleboats and the people staying up all night dancing and the lanterns and the gambling. The boys' eyes got bigger when Moses told them about blockading the harbor with those boats in the war.

Father rose, replaced his officer's hat, and walked through the sheep to us. The boys asked him about the war too, so he told them about Vicksburg. I was surprised. Father seldom spoke of the war, but here he didn't spare any of the details. He told about the weeks and weeks of the Union blockade and about finding the Confederates' mules gone, slaughtered for food and the harnesses used for food and an army without boots, defiant even when the surrendered, even though many could not stand they were so weak.

The boys didn't say much when Father finished. They had asked for stories of heroic charges and chases and smoky skirmishes. Father told them about starvation and deprivation and disease. Those boys might go on playing Johnny Reb and Billy Yank games, but they would never again have the feeling that what they played was what the war was like. Not after the blockade stories.

X

COOLER NIGHTS HELPED us herd the sheep better than we expected. It was our fifth Sunday away from home and we were already near a town called Canajoharie. We were finding more poplar trees and evergreens. Much of the land was cut over, with new juniper growth between the stumps.

But this day we were running into more marshland, making the travel more and more difficult in the dark.

"We'll begin traveling only by daylight," Father said. That would mean rising very early to begin our drives, going hard all day, and stopping just before dark to bed the sheep, set our camp, and scratch together our supper. Night was coming on earlier, and in another few weeks we would have more dark than light hours in the day. I wasn't eager to go all day without stopping, but the long uninterrupted sleeps would be a welcome change.

"We won't be able to explore as much along the river," Moses said.

"This is the hard work part Father meant," I said. "I reckon we can do it all right."

"We'll surely catch up to your Uncle Peter," Moses said.

"I think Father feels we will, but not because we're hurrying."

"Does he honestly believe the Lord will reward him for resting Sundays?" Moses asked.

"If he could have rested his troops Sundays, he would have," I said. "He says one reason the war took so long was the soldiers traded their religion for a rifle."

"What makes your father so religious and Uncle Peter not?" he asked.

"I guess he's religious because his brother isn't," I replied.

So we rested that Sunday and then began daylong driving of our sheep. It was very hard at first. Rising in the dark – we were used to that – but riding through the unforgiving heat of the day, that was hard. The terrain also grew rougher – stumps or cut trees in fields, marshland and oxbow turns along the river. But Father kept to his new plan and soon we grew used to it.

The colder nights were easier to tolerate as well. Being wrapped up in blankets asleep was better than wrapped up on horseback, still shivering and falling asleep in the saddle or dropping the wagon reins.

We saw fewer signs of muskrats, deer and bear during the day, and towns seemed to be smaller and farther apart. Maybe it was the soil that was poor or the drought, but farms looked less prosperous. The farm children stood and watched us without waving or running alongside the wagon or chasing the sheep. Fewer farms had sheep or horses in the pastures. Some had milk cows and chickens. Many barns needed roofs.

Father tried to sell sheep in Mohawk, but the price was so poor he decided better. If it weren't for John Dark Sky, we would have had to slaughter sheep ourselves. We still had the better part of the boar packed in salt, but Father was saving that for winter. Every day John Dark Sky was up before us, hunting. Moses and I were tired at the end of the day, too tired to help much by fishing. When we did get up with John Dark Sky, on those days, we caught bluegills and, on occasion, a small trout or two or three, but John Dark Sky shot rabbits, squirrels, and once he brought us a large turtle that we baked. John Dark Sky had baked turtles before, when Father was away, but this was so much better. We were hungrier, yes, but I thought this baked turtle was as good as any roast of venison.

"You're eating more now, both of you," Father said, "because you're growing. Soon we'll have to buy you larger boots and shirts."

It was true. My shirt was tight on me. I thought it had shrunk from being in and out of water so much, but it was my growing, not my clothes shrinking.

I secretly wanted moccasins like John Dark Sky's. He had made a pair for me when he took care of me during the war. They were too small for me now. But I knew Father preferred us to have boots. It would be boots then.

Sitting astride father's horse, surrounded by one hundred and forty sheep with their heads down except for one or two calling to one another and stirring up dust, I felt as though I were riding on a cloud. Moses nodded on the seat beside Father. John Dark Sky rode on the other side of the wagon, looking to the north. The wagon was a chariot under a punishing sun. All through the days, we rode without talking to each other, except to change rider and horseback and back to ride on the chariot as we led the sheep west.

Towards Ilion, Moses stood on the wagon seat to better see a column of smoke we were watching. As we drew closer, the sun was blotted out by the smoke and the noise, a roaring like the railroad, except that the rails ran south of us and this noise was coming from the north. Our eyes began to smart and Father raised his hand and stopped. I called the dogs to halt the sheep. They must have expected the sheep to comply, as the sheep had complied along the rivers noontimes.

But the sheep were restless and kicked at the dogs. The dogs nipped back and barked, continuing the noise. "It's a brush fire, a big one," Father said. "I'll go to the town to see if there is need for us."

We waited one hour, with John Dark Sky, continuing to watch the clouds of gray smoke rise. There was a strong smell of burning. Moses worried that there was danger in staying. Finally the sheep settled down to grazing.

"The wind is steady to the west," John Dark Sky said, "and we are one mile from the river and the town. The fire will not come this way. We might help the town before we leave."

Father returned, his face and his clothes sooty. "The town has burned to the river. The fields around the town are black and the animals are running." He told of some animals running into the flames. "We cannot help the people unless it is to stay to rebuild the town."

It was a sorry fact, but Father knew it was necessary to pass the town in its need. We went on, smelling the smoke all day. The fire had taken a very great toll and nothing would change that. We turned southward midmorning and then proceeded west through a wooded glen. It was a good thing the wind did not bring the fire to these woods or these fine, first-growth pines would have been destroyed. And how would we then have found a way through with the sheep?

We stopped and pitched a camp on the edge of the forest. John Dark Sky was cutting rawhide for laces to hold down the flaps of our lean-to. Soon the cold would set in. It was hard to think about cold. The sun was down and the cicadas were noisy and the heat still rose from the bare ground.

The next morning, Father used the last of our water for coffee. We were south of the Mohawk River considerable now, to skirt Ilion which was still burning, and we would not strike the river again for another day. If it had not been for the ewes and their milk, I don't know how we would have kept thirst from overcoming us. The sun rose in a smoky haze through the woods behind us. But ashes from Ilion did not spread as far south as where we were.

Last night's rabbit stew thinned with sheep's milk was still warm and tasted better than porridge. I guess it was my growing. The same stew would not have appealed to me a year before. Even the milky coffee tasted fine.

As Moses and I packed the bedrolls and the cooking pot into the wagon, a tawny cat appeared between the spokes of the wheels. Cats meant people, but we hadn't seen or heard any signs of others.

John Dark Sky looked hard into the woods all around us and then at the pine needles beneath us. A bearded man dressed in deerskins wandered into our camping circle and stood next to our wagon. Tanned deerskins and hides lay stacked on the back shelf of the wagon. John Dark Sky placed the skin he was cutting on the ground near the remains of our cookfire.

"Hello," said Father. "Would you care for some coffee made with sheep's milk?"

The man clad in deerskins said nothing. He looked at us for a moment more; then he reached over and rubbed the topmost deerskin. He went through this procedure again, slowly fingering the nap of each hide. He seemed not to be looking at them, merely touching them, his eyes somewhere else. He said nothing.

John Dark Sky walked over to the wagon. The man withdrew his hand. John Dark Sky reached over to the stack of hides and pulled one out from the middle, using both hands. He held it out to the wanderer.

The man did not look at John Dark Sky's offering. He was looking past John Dark Sky's outreached hands. He still said nothing.

Then he moved. Past John Dark Sky, past the wagon, over to the fire where Moses had been watching John Dark Sky cut the deerskin into laces. Moses moved aside for the man who came right over to the half-cut hide that lay on the ground. He looked down at it. Then he bent down and rubbed all along its edges, down the cut edge and across the length of what was left of the hide.

He stood up holding the half-cut hide and looked back into the woods. The cat came over and rubbed between his legs. Then the man, still holding the cut deerskin in both hands, walked back past John Dark Sky and into the woods in the direction we had come the day before.

Father stood looking after him. The little cat unwound itself from the spokes of our wagon wheel and trotted off after the man with the leather skin. Our dogs had not barked, nor had John Dark Sky seemed to sense the leatherman's arrival. But when he appeared, I wasn't frightened. We all accepted his presence as if he had been a ghost. Perhaps he came and went so quietly people weren't sure if he was there or not. I wouldn't have been aware of him except for stories about him I'd heard. As we returned John Dark Sky's hides to their place and finished packing up the wagon, Moses said, "We aren't so much different from that leatherman."

"How so?" I asked.

"Well, he is a wanderer; so are we. He lives off the land and so do we. We eat the game John Dark Sky shoots and use the hides."

I handed him the washed coffee pot and tin cups that were now dry. "Yes, but he depends on everyone else. We're independent."

"We depend on other people all day," he said. "On each other. On your father."

"But if anything happened, we wouldn't become hermits. We could still talk to others."

"It might be we could. I hope we never find out," he said.

With little time to spare before sunset, we crossed a dried river flat, climbed a rise and raced pell-mell down to the banks and into the shoals of the Mohawk River. The water was shallow here near Utica and warm. Three different flocks of Canada geese and flocks of ducks lifted up, circled, and reestablished themselves downstream.

Father made a fire and he and John Dark Sky went about collecting the stray sheep that hadn't gone to the river's edge. If we were to have a supper tonight other than jerky and milk, Moses and I would have to provide it.

While I put up the lean-to and tied back the flaps with the new rawhide laces, Moses fetched down our fishing poles from the wagon and dug into the leaf mold along the river's edge for worms. Soon we were wading into the river, boots and all, with the daylight all but gone and heat lightning pulsing to the north.

A few carp took our worms and we threw them back. One foot-long sucker swallowed my hook. I didn't disengage it but left the dying fish on my line and anchored my pole in the crotch of a tree while I reached for Moses' new hook to tie onto my line.

Moses yanked my arm and pointed with the tip of his pole. The sucker disappeared and my line began sawing back and forth, up and down the ripples near shore.

"What is it? I whispered.

"I think a turtle took your sucker."

"I'm going to get it off," I said and reached from my pole.

"No, don't. Wait for a minute. I might not be a turtle, Jesse," he said.

"Well, I don't care what it is. I'm hungry. Let's go back," and I hefted my pole.

I thought, from the slow tugging, that the line had become ensnared. "I have a snag," I said, moving downstream. But just as I reached the ripples where I thought my line was snagged, a dark shape rushed through the shallows and bumped my leg, sailing past, nearly unending me. I spun around, then threw my arms back to regain my balance when my line tripped me face forward into the water.

I managed to hold onto my pole and Moses splashed over to help me up. He caught hold of my line and scooped it in. It slackened. Whatever was on the end was propelling itself back toward us.

It went by Moses who lunged at it, but missed. It came around heading straight for me. I was still down in the water on all fours. I rose halfway up and hurdled out of the water and drove both boot heels down onto the back of a huge fish as it passed beneath me and I tumbled backwards this time into the shallow water.

Then Moses was on top of my legs and we both made a grab for the fish. Moses hooked one hand in a heaving gill flap and I scissored the fish with my legs and hugged its thrashing flanks.

It snapped an enormous tail fin back and forth, nearly throwing both of us off, but Moses reached his hand deep into the gill flap and ripped the entire right side set of gills out, bring the sucker halfway out with the gills and popping the fish's innards partway out.

A final lashing of that huge tail and the fish was calm, floating sideways, half its insides pulled into its throat, leaving a depression in the stomach cavity.

We pulled the fish ashore and look at its full length, finally. Moses was the first to regain his breath.

"Bet it's twenty pounds anyway," he laughed, exhausted.

I still had hold of my pole, but the line was hopelessly twisted around the tail. "What is it?" I asked.

"It's a whale," Moses said.

Slowly, we brought the fish back to the campfire, Moses holding the gills and I held the tail up by my tangled line.

Father saw us coming into the light of the fire. "Is one of the dogs hurt? No, my stars, what did you catch? John!" He called across the flock of sheep to John Dark Sky's silhouette against the heat lightning. John Dark Sky came through the sheep into the firelight.

A look of greatest delight crossed his face and he looked at the fish. "Muskellunge," he said. "You have a big fish. Which one caught it?"

"I did!" we both spoke at once.

"We both did," I said, holding the tail up.

"It's twenty pounds if it's an ounce," Father said. "Let's clean it and steak it for tonight. Tomorrow we can salt it. This is a fine fish."

Father filleted the long sides of the muskie and we washed the two pieces thoroughly in the river. When we returned to the fire, John Dark Sky had the skillet going with lard sizzling.

XI

UTICA WAS THE northernmost town we struck, but it was the hottest. The weather turned so blazing we had to return to long periods of rest during the days. Most shade trees along the Mohawk River bad been cleared here in Utica. The land down to the river was scraped clean of hardwood. It made our midday travel next to impossible. Father drove the wagon along the river roads that began to widen as we came more into the center of Utica in the morning.

In spite of the hot weather, Utica's waterfront market was lively with farmers trading crops and purchasing goods brought to town on the railroad. Pens containing hogs, sheep and cattle bordered the river, where large flatboats were tied to pilings.

Citizens of Utica seemed used to such hot days, but I felt faint. There was no shelter anywhere for the sheep, and Father did not want to pen them in full sun, so we drove the flock on through town and found a mill a mile outside of town with a few second growth maples and pines along the millstream. While the sheep scratched places into the soft pine needles to rest, we watered the horses and mules. Father spoke to the miller about Uncle Peter and Cotton. They had brought their sheep to this same mill two weeks before, so we had not gained on them, or if we had, we lost ground again in the forest south of Ilion.

Moses and I walked to town to show off our muskie head. The rows of its teeth were sharp and the head alone weighed nearly one half pound. We had been lucky to avoid battle scars.

Two boys outside the schoolyard stopped wrestling and ran up to see what Moses was showing to their younger brothers.

"I never saw a trout that big!" one younger boy said.

"That's not a trout, it's a muskie," one boy corrected. "It's that big muskie your daddy's been trying to catch, Billy."

"Where'd you catch him?" a red-haired boy demanded.

"Down river. Near Frankfort," I said. "It was the biggest fish we ever caught." I knew enough to play humble.

"Yeah," said the redhead, "but my daddy's caught bigger."

Even though I knew Moses had caught bigger catfish, I kept pretending this was a behemoth and we had been blessed.

"Whadja use for bait?" a girl in overalls and pigtails asked.

"A sucker," Moses said. "It swallowed the whole sucker and that's how we got it."

"It didn't break your line?"

"You didn't break your pole?"

And questions like those kept coming. Even some adults looked over and pointed as they talked.

We kept answering the questions and telling the story of the battle over and over. The children referred to Moses and me as those shepherd boys. We never got to buy any candy or try their hoops game because they wanted to hear every detail of the battle again and again.

Finally, Father came and ushered us off with him on the wagon. He had sold five sheep and restocked our dwindling supplies. We dined on smoked ham and sweet potatoes for supper.

I stayed awake and began to write down some of the things we had done. It was going on our seventh week, and I wanted to get it all down about the railroad and river traffic and the fish and the leatherman and people in Albany and Utica before I forgot any.

The mill was a fine place to stay, but we had become used to traveling. The sheep expected it. Six, almost seven full weeks of marching evenings, and then morning and afternoons, and now evenings again put us in a spirit of moving. I wasn't sure, but I thought I had probably slept some days in the saddle on Father's horse. I'm certain I had fallen asleep on the gently rocking wagon, next to Father or next to John Dark Sky while Father rode.

The river was also something we were used to seeing. But it was always different. The Hudson was there every day at home, but this Mohawk River was ever changing. We seemed to move more quickly against the flow of its water. And we drank it. The Mohawk was shallower, bending more than the Hudson, its power harnessed by mills like the one we were now preparing to leave behind in Utica. We slept to the sound of the water rushing through the mill and we bathed in its green color.

"Do you think this river freezes all the way across in the winter?" Moses asked when he awoke.

"I do, but let's ask," I said. But of course if the Hudson froze almost across in Esopus, this Mohawk River would surely freeze. We asked the miller.

"You'll find the ice house in every town up the Mohawk River," he said and patted a large saw with an ice blade hanging in his shed. "We use this when the millpond freezes here, and the lumber mill has some bigger," the miller said. "The mill's ice's all but gone in this heat, but there's still some chunks in the ice house in town."

The town ice house, next to the railyard, stored ice not the green color of the river but black like the Hudson ice, as if it had trapped a gloomy Utica sky in its core.

We did not buy any ice, but we stopped back in town to post Father's letter to Sarah before we left.

4 Nov, 1863

Dear Sarah,

We are already in Utica, New York, ahead of our itinerary. Peter and Cotton are ahead of us and reported to be well by townspeople along our way. There is game enough, though we have sold a dozen sheep for supplies. Moses and Jesse have helped by surprising us with fish.

John Dark Sky is well as are we all, and he sends you his regards.

By Christmas, we should be in Pennsylvania. Please offer our greetings to the Friends. We shall forward greetings to the Friends Meeting in Erie. We continue to see Friends Meetings, but no town we have struck Sundays has had a meetinghouse. We commune with the Lord's spirit every day and keep the Sabbath for rest.

Please convey our gratitude to the Baxters for their hospitality. You may rest assured that they are willing to help with our harvest as are others in the Kingston meeting.

We wish you and Ruth the best of health and Godspeed for Cotton's safe return We all hope for the same. Remaining yours,

Fondly,
John L. Stiles

The sun set a brilliant golden path before us as we left the mill and headed on to Lake Oneida. A cooling in the evening lent more liveliness to our pace,

The river's breadth increased as the night wore on. We rested later than usual the next day and spent the rest of that day watching steamboats towing barges up the river to Utica. As we were setting off that evening, one steamer returned, moving rapidly downstream.

We hailed the captain who shouted to us that the river fed into Lake Oneida not many miles west. That morning, our canvas fly on the near side of the wagon gave us shade as we went along, and the tarpaulin overhead protected us from the rays of the sun. After we gathered the sheep for the evening, Moses was so tired of entertaining the town children that he went right to sleep after supper.

XII

It was not yet light when we came through a small village called Rome. Here, the Mohawk River went north, and here we began to follow the barge canal the rest of the way to Oneida Lake, another half day's journey according to a man walking his mule to town.

Even though it was early in the day, we set camp on the western side of Rome but didn't build a fire. We had come a long way and were too tired to go back into town to see whether it looked like our idea of ancient Rome.

"Rome. Another forum," Moses said sleepily as he pulled his shirt off and went down to the waterway to bathe.

I understood what Moses meant. My enthusiasm had dimmed, explaining our journey over and over to town children back in Fultonville and Utica. I stretched out and fell asleep thinking about the circumstances Mrs. Farr, our classics teacher, had read to us about Roman slaves, not as discouraging as our slavery, but I declined nevertheless to go into Rome, New York.

I guess it was close to four in the afternoon when I awoke, stiff from having slept on the ground only on a blanket laid out in the shade of the wagon. Father was cutting jerky for our supper. John Dark Sky found watercress along one of the streams feeding the canal and made a sort of salad using dandelion greens and watercress and onion grasses.

I had a keen appetite and it tasted good. Our sheep's milk was always good tasting. Father sliced some of the ham with his Barlow knife.

It was a simple meal but would be enough to keep us until we made a bigger camp the next day, on the shore of Oneida Lake, another several miles Father guessed.

When we traded watch rotation at midnight, I had a gnawing hunger and chewed slices of jerky to keep the pangs away until morning. I tugged at the jerky into the early morning hours, both to keep awake and fend off the empty feeling in my stomach.

A coolness settled in as we roused the sheep. Shivering woke me out of a reverie on Boca, and he too might have been asleep walking among the slowmoving flock. The land in the distance was black, not the usual blue-gray, and a mist rose over all.

It became not land at all but a large lakeshore, cooling in the early morning air, steam rising off the water like a dream.

With the sheep drinking at the lake's edge, we went about making a more official camp – a fire, the fly of the wagon staked out, the mules hobbled, and sleeping pallets spread out for the morning rest.

But Moses was not about to rest. He raced down to the lake's edge to wade in and look for turtles. He was like a boy beholding Santa Claus. It was embarrassing, but Father just laughed. I went on the chores – tethering the horses and unpacking the kettle and the other cooking things. When I went to the edge of the lake, away from where Moses was churning up the sand, I glared over at him. He was positively useless, throwing wet sand up in the air and letting it fall on his shirt. "Moses!" I called when I could stand the sight no longer. "Where's your dignity?"

"Must be I unlearned dignity a little back at the boar's nest," he said, sending a comet of sand my way.

Then I don't know what got into me. I was running at him in knee deep water. "Growling," Moses said later, after we prayed for forgiveness. Times like those Father made us do so. And I was pummeling him, only I couldn't see what I was doing the hot tears were so blinding.

"And I was just grabbing your arms and missed and caught you on the ear," Moses explained in all certitude.

My ear still stung, and I gather I had lost more in the dignity category. What Moses did in words had unlocked all the fury of the sow's charge and added it to my sorrow over our dead dog and the sow and piglets and the nearness of my own death and my failure to act and the whole unending weariness of the journey.

"Well, we both have a little to learn if we are to repel any boars' charges," I said. I could laugh at it, after that prayer begging forgiveness. "Unless boars have as sensitive ears as mine and you can stop 'em with one wallop."

After cleaning up the supper and returning the kettle to the wagon, Moses and I set about cutting the cattails growing along the shore of Oneida Lake. These stalks also grew in abundance along the marshy streams feeing into the lake. It was my idea, but Moses leapt on it and took it over, adding the Christmas present suggestion.

"Let's cut the cattails and make a mat to sleep on," I said. That is how it started.

"Let's make your Father and John Dark Sky presents of them," Moses said. "For Christmas. We could hide them in the wagon and work on them nights and Sundays."

So it became his idea. And he went about it full of himself, romping through the marsh and snapping the cattail grasses. This time, I felt it too, following him through the marshes. We spent an hour collecting cattails, another hour to begin the weaving, and, after dark, we rolled what we had woven together and strapped the rolls under the wagon flooring in back. For days afterward, every chance we could, we would weave more of the mats. Two Sundays would pass before they were as finished as we could make them, without tying them off and stitching them. They weren't proud like Sarah's, but we had two fitting presents for Father and John Dark Sky, come Christmas.

And I think it pleased Father to see us working so closely on a project, so he must have thought his prayer had been answered. And maybe it had been. I can't argue that.

We had been gone too long for me to keep track of days. I'd lost count in my journal and simply recorded the main things like the fire in Ilion and catching the muskellunge.

October brought changes – cooler days. We were all right circling Oneida Lake daytimes now. It wasn't Sunday, but Father said we could rest one whole day and all that night, that being rested wasn't going to cost us time.

So we lay awake by the firs in the first actually cool evening we could remember since Esopus. We talked about the farm, whether any of the corn had grown back. "I doubt it could have," said Father, "but I would not put it past Sarah to have some to harvest, somehow." And about the other crops, the apples and the fall raspberry crop. About the school we were missing and when we would see our friends again.

"We should see Baxters on the way back," Moses hoped. He thought he had won Susan's heart.

"We might find you a pretty Wisconsin maiden," I said. Perhaps the Harrisons have a daughter our age. Of course, for you, six- or seven-year-old young ladies would do just as well," I had to add.

"Six or seven daughters, yes."

Father and John Dark Sky studied Oneida Lake to determine whether to go north around it or follow the southern shoreline. A number of wagon trails had gone south, and Father was for following those. "That is the way Peter would have gone."

But for some reason, the next morning he was persuaded to go north. "And cross the barge canal later on."

So on a cooler day than we had yet had the pleasure of riding into, we broke camp, rounded up the sheep, and began our skirting of Oneida Lake to the north, towards the town of Cleveland on the northern shore, the only Cleveland we would strike on our journey.

If there had been few towns and poor farms along the road from Utica, there were none on the north road of Oneida Lake. The water, reflecting a green shoreline, glistened in the morning breeze. Whitecaps slapped the shore where the road touched the lake. The steady wind caused us to pull on our shirts and button them up to the neck to keep warm, something I was unaccustomed to. And it was none too comfortable. My shirt had indeed grown too small for me at the neck and the sleeves were hard to button.

Moses offered to give me his shirt. So he could wear one of John Dark Sky's jackets, I was willing to bet. I took him up on it and felt much warmer with the looser fit his shirt afforded. Moses did wear one of the leather jackets and looked proud as can be.

XIII

DAYTIME TRAVEL MEANT my getting up early, before sunup now, unless I was up already and on watch. I would poke up the fire and see John Dark Sky ride out to scout our trail. With fortune on our side, John Dark Sky would shoot a quail or a rabbit. Then it was preparing morning food for the four of us. The job was Father's, but I wished for Cotton's cooking. Still, the crackling of a fire and the smell of coffee made it pleasant to be alive.

Moses and I had the job of shaking blankets and rolling bedding to stow in the wagon. I got out the cook skillet and tin plates and cups while Moses fetched more water to wash the utensils afterward.

I also checked harnesses and fed the horses and mules, if there had been too few grasses for grazing. Moses collected any clothes we had hung out to dry the night before. Both of us were clothes washers, if we found ourselves near enough to water. And we had been, pretty steadily, alongside the Mohawk River and now, Oneida Lake.

Oneida Lake had no stones along the shore to rub the grime out of our pants and socks, so Moses and I used sand and I rinsed the things as much as I thought they needed rinsing. Still, upon plucking the clothes off the branches where they dried overnight, a sprinkling of sand fell out of the fibers.

"Better shake those out well," said Father as he stood nearby looking at the sky. "I prefer not to have sand in my boots if there's any walking to be done."

"Might be sand, but these are cleaner than before, Father," I said.

"For the cleaner, I'm obliged deeply," he said. And that was all.

I shook the sand and brushed it out till the nap of the clothing was loose. I do believe the beach where we camped was a bit higher than it had been before I commenced my shaking out of the clothes.

Our procession wound through the lakeside towns along the northern shore, Cleveland and Constantia, to the westernmost point where the Oswego River fed into Oneida Lake. Most of the citizens of these towns were farmers, but at Brewerton, where the lake curved around south again, mule drivers and lockkeepers and bargemen milled around outside a tavern. They were a rough looking crew. Mr. Baxter was right about that. But they spoke to us about the traffic and the conditions of the roads and towpath on the canal in a friendly enough manner

We talked at length to one bearded man with a booming voice, a captain on a steamboat that towed the barges from the mouth of the canal across Oneida Lake to the Mohawk's mouth for further towing, or to dock in Brewerton for unloading, or sometime, he said, for towing up the Mohawk to Utica or farther. He told us that canalmen were the best workers, notwithstanding their gruff manner. "They'll work thirty hours straight, rest five, then go another day and take their meals on the go. And these bargemen here are supposed to be letting the young whippersnappers do all the toting. The war put all the young ones into uniform and pressed these fellows back to lifting and hauling."

"Do the crews operate Sundays too?" Father asked him about Sundays, sure enough.

"Sundays too the captain said. "I don't go out myself. But the canal traffic has to clear, so the crews keep it flowing every day. I can make up the difference, tow all the waiting barges by Tuesday, sometimes Wednesday, but I take Sunday or any bad weather day for catching up on the log and the billing."

"I admire you for that," Father said.

"The older crews seem rowdy, but you can't fault the men and say they are not working hard. You can't begrudge them their time to restore their gumption. They stop in at the tavern here and talk about their hard lives and make fun of each other in harsh ways, it seems. But when their barge ships out, they are ready for her and will take her straight to Buffalo if needs be. You can't beat a bargeman for sticking to his task."

"My shepherd crew here has been going eight weeks nearly, Sundays excepted," Father said with genuine pride. "They are ready for the next six-week stretch to Buffalo and they don't require any of the talk that I hear yonder."

One of the mule drivers was being set upon by a steersman, railing at him and poking him in the midriff with a piece of broken tiller. Two other barge crewmen were cheering the steersman. The mule driver let out a howl as the tiller smote his legs. Someone from the doorway ran over and handed him a bullwhip, and the steersman fetched the driver's savior a blow athwart his back.

Before the steersman could turn back to his first victim, the mule driver had unfurled the whip and cracked it once like a pistol shot next to the steersman's ear. Another crack set the steersman back on his heels to avoid the blow. The mule driver coiled the whip around the steersman's boot and upended him in the dust.

Instead of lashing the helpless steersman, the mule driver merely coiled his whip, glared at the man lying in the dust, turned with a curse on the man and his descendants, and walked back into the tavern.

Cheers went up in the tavern as the driver returned.

"That's about as rough as it gets," said the tugboat captain. "Those men depend on each other day in and day out. They might be rough on each other here, but they don't let harm come to any of them on the river. That one with the tiller needed his comeuppance, and he might have deserved more. But the mule driver, the one with the whip, didn't dare to harm him. Sooner or later he will need him and every other man and beast on the canal. There's none that can let another down. Especially in these times."

The steersman picked himself up and spat in the dust. His two crew mates led him over to a rainbarrel and splashed water in his face. Then they led him down the street toward the docks.

The scene at the Breweton tavern plagued me because I felt I had been to blame for my brawl with Moses. Now I saw that men who were justifiably enemies, for whatever insult or injury, would not really harm each other. And I had been ready to bring harm to Moses.

Was I evil? Did I have a vengeful nature? Could I even go to war and not become a murderer?

I found no answers, and I still have no answers. All along the Erie Canal bargeway, I found much time to think about such things, with day after day's hard labor a testimony to the harsh lives of the barge crews.

We witnessed the most severe of physical tasks, with barges laden with ore being pulled along narrow channels, even bumping the sides at times, a team of mules stretched to the limits of their strength and endurance by men who would take no rest, mile after mile, day after day, along a two hundred mile sluice that offered little shade to the barge crew, little rest to the mule team or driver till they arrived at a lock.

My own endurance paled next to such efforts. My own thoughts turned to my being inadequate to the task of driving the sheep alongside the canal. We had such an easy task compared to canalboaters. And I was so weary every day, even sitting in the wagon.

Nights we camped alongside the canal, chilled by the lengthening evening dews, hearkening to the boisterous songs and laughter of barge crews. Occasionally one of the crew would stop by our campfire to talk or hear about life south of Albany. We welcomed these visits. The stories the canalboaters told were colorful, harsh reflections of their lives. They differed from our stories only in degree, it seemed, with ours being a slice milder than theirs.

Were we preparing for some harsher tasks ahead? Were these stories and the tests of strength and endurance we overheard the same harsh stories of our road farther to the west? Was it the West what made these men who they were? I felt myself becoming harder hearted. I wasn't sure I could accept my mean-spirited feelings and what they might lead to, but I could not deny they were there. This too may have been the harder part of the journey that Father meant.

Newark and Macedon and Fairport were ports where we stopped Sundays. The days became much cooler, and some sprinkling of rain kept our progress westward at a pace that pleased Father. Even downpours of rain did not dampen his spirits.

My spirits were slipping. The endless canal, always extending into the horizon, a lame mule to add to our lame dog, my own aches from sitting stride Boca or seated on the wagon had limits.

Our meat rations dwindled to near nothing, and although we could slaughter sheep, we did not. The barge crews were amply fixed with beans, flour, turnips and potatoes as well as tea and coffee. Their cooks seemed glad to accept our greenbacks for surplus from their stores, and so we found enough to supplement our meals. Apple trees had been planted in number along the canal too, and we found picking the juicy red fruit a pleasing distraction evenings.

John Dark Sky found less and less game, scarcely any rabbits, and nary a squirrel. The only game was an occasional grouse or partridge, but nothing to sink your teeth into. Moses and I found few fish in the canal, only panfish in occasional streams feeding into it.

The canal did produce something beside the barge kitchens fare – excellent frogs. We found their legs sweet, better than the game John Dark Sky brought in. Five or six big bullfrogs made enough for three of us. John Dark Sky would not eat them. He preferred deer jerky or a bird or the rabbit he might have shot.

Early in the eleventh week along the westward journey, after we rested all of a Sunday at a lock in Freeport, we began to hear the canal talk of Rochester. Word came of the great Lake Ontario just north of Rochester and of the large railroad switching yards. The Oswego River sounded more like a real river, not this narrow canal we had to travel.

I begged Father to allow a day up the Oswego River to see the great lake, but he pointed out our plan to follow an even bigger body of water, Lake Erie, when we reached Buffalo, a few weeks hence. I would have to delay seeing Lake Ontario until we returned.

XIV

AT HOME, A harvest season always brings out the best preserved fruit and baking. I was sure the harvests here in Western New York would yield the same. We saw families haying the fields and apple picking. Small pyramids of pumpkins and squashes began to appear at the landings in baskets next to which stood a child with the box of pennies, nickels and dimes. We bought cider and honeycomb to go with our spoon bread and pancakes, and John Dark Sky sold some of his deerskins.

The trees were motley, more yellows as the days passed, from the sassafras and beech and rock maples, Father said, but mixed in with the green juniper and pine and red and green, half-turned silver maple second growth. It was an earlier fall turning-of-the-trees here. Our trees would turn soon, but the only browns here were oak and ash that had dried out and changed fast and clung to their leaves.

It seemed a cooler fall than Esopus falls up here as well. Whole days I kept my shirt on and it wasn't December yet. These were days Moses looked cold until mid-morning and he stayed wrapped in his blanket for up to an hour when he was on wagon detail, even wearing John Dark Sky's leather coat.

The road we took V-ed away from the canal and along the ridge of a sandy hill with briars growing down the north-facing side. A line of brightly colored trees in the distance marked the riverbed we had been expecting, and John Dark Sky's horse and Boca perked up their nostrils as they scented water.

We arrived at the Oswego River midday. I was already weary from a long morning up on Boca, and I had to free a ewe from brambles where her long wool had tangled. When I dismounted to snip the snarls of wool, I could hardly stand straight and I couldn't straighten up again when we stopped at the Oswego River.

Father hopped off the wagon and came over to help me up. Even with his support, I was cramped up too badly to stand straight. My feet were tingling from having been asleep, unlike the rest of me. I sat back down and pulled off my boots to rub my toes.

"I wager the stirrup setting is up too high," Father said, and he lowered the lines to the creased mark where his legs fit the stirrups. "Here you are, Jesse, full length for you from now on."

I was as tall as Father, unlikely as it seemed, almost eye to eye now. I put my boots back on and hobbled over to help Moses round up the sheep to cross the river.

The sandy hills along the riverbank were easy to slide down into the water, but the cold water cramped my legs again, I stood up in the stirrups to stretch them out as the clear running water swirled around my boots. "You look ten feet tall!" Moses exclaimed as he looked up from the wagon seat as it swung by in the current.

When all the sheep were across and the wagon, forded, the ruts in the roadbed took two directions. One was a mule path leading upstream. "That goes to the lake, I surmise," Father said. Barges to and from the lake were towed on this path, but none were moving this noonday.

The other road, the one we were taking, climbed a steep bank, and when we reached the top, we saw Rochester beyond in the sunlight. "The sky's smoked up from steam locomotives," Moses said. As he surmised, the rails we came upon led away from the center of the town where the canal joined the Oswego River as the river curled north again.

At the junction of the canal and the Oswego River a maze of rails and road went off in many directions. Three silos rose up alongside the rails and a roundhouse and water towers blocked the tree line. Where the river widened, long piers jutted out into the water and along them rails with open top hopper cars were waiting to have grain shoveled out onto waiting barges. But the noon hour brought everything to a halt. Everything except the steam locomotives that idled with smoke hanging over the black and silver stacks. The still scene seemed poised for a signal when we herded the sheep through the confusion of crates, across sets of rails and along the riverbank. Brakemen and engine drivers sat at their noon meals on benches, or stood, leaning again the roundhouse, smoking and watching us pass.

Father pulled the mules to a halt next to one cluster of railroad and canal crews. He got down from the wagon and stood speaking to the crewmen as we rode by. We recognized some of the canal crew and waved. They waved back, smug at having beaten us to Rochester, I was certain.

A mile beyond the switching yard, past where the rails bridged across the canal and turned west, the canal angled north again. Father rode up and we gathered the sheep around the wagon and stopped for our own noon meal.

This time, my legs were solid under me and my feet were not numb. "The stirrups did it," I said, thanking Father.

"Next your boots will be too small, and you will have outgrown your pants by Christmas," he laughed. But he was proud I was growing, I could tell.

We took an extra hour of rest, oiling a new harness Father bought, brushing out the burs from the dogs' fur, and spreading the bedding out to sun. Father opened the bundles of winter clothes. "You may find these will come in handy shortly," he said. And he took lined gloves and woolen scarves and sweaters from a bundle that smelled of camphor.

We had been using whale oil for lamps, but Father had sold some and wanted to save some for a present for the Harrisons, so we used the rest sparingly. He'd bought a container of kerosene, cheaper and smokier, but just as safe for the lamps. We'd have to clean the stacks more often now, but the whale oil was an especially fine house present, we knew.

An endless string of small landings occurred, "ports" the local citizenry called them. But port to us meant Poughkeepsie, and Albany and Kingston. Spencerport and Rockport were one-dock ports, a few barge slips, not berths for steamboats, no ferry landing, no bridges over the canal. Moses was kinder than I had ever seen him to praise each small village, and he was eloquent in admiration of the bustle in each sleepy landing. Usually there was an older lockkeeper, or his wife collecting the tariff, her family laundry hanging along the dock.

For weeks, a month, into the coldest weather of our trip with frost on the fields in the morning and steam rising off the canal, we plodded along, through Albion, the only canal town with running water, and Medina, barely three small houses and a storage barn besides the lock, and on to Lockport, where the train ran a spur up to the canal again, and where we stopped for a day.

A newspaper Father bought in Lockport told us what we suspected. President Lincoln was declaring this last Thursday in November National Day of Thanks to "our beneficent father" for the blessing of our land. Peace was the most blessed prayer. Father had prayed for peace, upon his return from Washington, and asked now again, "Peace be in our time, O Lord, and safety to those with whom we cannot celebrate together."

Where were Uncle Peter and Cotton this Thanksgiving Day? Perhaps in Pennsylvania now. We hadn't heard any news and the canal report of them had stopped the week before, so they had left the barge canal, passed through Buffalo and were somewhere beside Lake Erie.

All day long this Thanksgiving Day, the Lockport townspeople and farmers from the countryside gathered to celebrate. It was like the Pilgrims – Thanksgiving with wild turkeys on spits in the town square, jars of preserves standing open, cider and beer flowing. The canal workers gathered, beards combed, and thanked the Lord their Maker, holding hands with farmers and with us, Father in his uniform, in common celebration. We ate until we felt sluggish then helped return the townspeople's tables to houses and pass leftover food around to be taken to their houses. When the square was again empty, Moses and I lay on benches in the last of the sunlight.

I wrote in my journal about the festivities the fine people of Lockport had shared with all of their neighbors. I vowed to welcome all the travelers who stopped by our farm in Esopus. It was a small enough response to our blessings on this trip, I thought.

Moses began a journal as well, only he was writing his in French. "In case we go to Canada," he said, "or run into trappers who speak French."

"Or in case you need a code to keep pirates from tracing your steps," I said.

Pirates, brigands, warmongers, they all seemed far away. Except that there were no young men on the canal or in the towns. There would be a handful, some missing limbs like Uncle Peter, but most of the young men whom we might have encountered would not have been celebrating a Thanksgiving of peace. I was finally, especially thankful, eternally grateful that Father returned safely from the War. And I wrote a prayer that I would never have to fire a gun at any man.

XV

THE GREAT PORT of Buffalo loomed ahead hanging in the sky. Smoke rose from the chimneys into the gray cloud bank lowering overhead. Church steeples pricked the sky. The sky turned grayer as we drove the flock through Tonawanda Village, and the horizon as we came to the Niagara River looked angrier by the minute. Then the sky removed the rooflines like a coffin closing.

"A storm is heading our way," Father said, as we approached the railroad bridge. Wagons were crossing into Canada, disappearing in smoke as the railroad steamed across beneath. It was not cold like this earlier this morning, but the frost had been heavy. Moses now closed the leather coat at his waist and I put on my gloves.

Herds of cattle and pigs were waiting to cross to Canada. I could not make out the Canada shoreline where the bridge ended. The train disappeared into the lowering clouds, its smoke becoming one with the gray sky.

Father spoke to John Dark Sky but the wind covered his words. He leaned back over Boca's flanks and pointed south. "We will try to work along Lake Erie, south," were the words I could make out.

We went two miles only and stopped the sheep on a flat stretch where the river broadened into the lake. The other shore, the Canada shore, was barely visible. "Soon," Father said, "we will lose sight of the Canada shore." So I would not have my boots strike foreign soil this trip. Or perhaps ever.

We stopped again in town where two large roads merged. Two wagons, burdened with supplies, wheeled down the road in opposite directions. Other wagons were lined up at a feed store, unloading grain.

Wagons everywhere we looked were filling up with bags of flour, furs, beeves, and other supplies.

Father bought three bales of hay for the animals. He lifted the bales onto the wagon's lazy board, the only space available. "This will do for the time being, and we will ride double as long as the storm stays north. If it comes to us, we shall find a farm with a barn for shelter," he said. I thought about what we could eat if a storm set upon us and what shelter we would find.

The railroad yard was even more ahum with engines pulling flatcars loaded with logs along rails up from the river's edge, other engines standing with smoke rising from their stacks, and a large ferry waiting at dock, sending black billows from its stack into the overhanging clouds.

Barges, towed downriver from the canal, were towed slowly in twos and threes against the current, disappearing into the cloud cover, except for trails of black smoke from their tugs.

That Saturday morning, Father and John Dark Sky got out the so'westers for us and lashed the canvas side of the wagon tight. Small snowflakes drifted down into the river as we rounded up the flock after our noon meal. The wind picked up more still, blowing from behind us now and down along the river where it fed into the lake. Snow whitened the sky between us and the lakeshore and began to mat the thick wooly coats of the sheep. They would be all right. I pulled my scarf up over my head and put my hat firmly down over it to keep the wind off my back. Up on John Dark Sky's horse, riding behind him, Moses turned his collar up and tied his scarf about his neck and over him mouth. We set off through the traffic of Buffalo's rail yards, ferries, tugs and barges, and began our southward leg around Lake Erie.

It snowed the rest of that afternoon until father called a halt in a country churchyard. We had only traveled six miles. The wagon wheels kept sideslipping in the drifts and had to be pushed back onto the road. The mules had been wearying since three o'clock. Darkness was coming on, and the snow created even more difficulty seeing the road. We turned the wagon sideways into the wind on the lee side of a church.

The minister waved to us from his parsonage porch and pointed to his woodpile and shouted welcome, but he didn't come out into the weather.

His small house looked cheery, but there was no room beyond him and his wife the child who stood in the doorway, all three.

Moses and I went over to his porch when he came out to replenish his wood. He welcomed us again. "Your uncle, I believe, came by not two weeks ago and spent a Sunday night here. Gave us a jar of good whiskey, he did."

When Moses heard that, he hurried back through the snow to the wagon and brought the remains of one of our jars.

"Much obliged, but I'd best wait till tomorrow, after the sermon," the minister said. He thanked us and offered to have us come in, but we mentioned we would watch the sheep and gave him greetings from father. He thanked us again and bid us stay as long as we wished. He said his congregation would not be coming in from farms for Sunday service in this weather. Instead, he said he would hold service for us the next morning, and we thanked him and said we would be appreciative.

It was a congregational service and not wholly different from the Quaker Meeting except we sang hymns and only the minister spoke. He thanked us for attending and prayed for our safe journey, and Father put two coins in the offering place in the narthex, where our overcoats were hung drying.

The snow was turning to rain as we returned to the wagon. Our coats were soon soaked again and the snow on the sheep's coats turned to slurry. There would be no passage on the road unless the weather turned warmer, or unless the ground froze firmly so that the wagon wheels could cart us on along Lake Erie's shore.

All night the rain beat down on our wagon. We huddled inside, even John Dark Sky, waiting out the weather. Once, I woke up to hear a noise like someone knocking on the canvas top, and yet it was not firm enough to knock on the canvas, and the fly was up anyway, so how could there be anyone knocking?

And then it was morning and John Dark Sky was breaking outward the canvas fly Father had secured to the top and one side of the wagon. A crystalline world seen as if through tears clicked awake. Icicles from the sheep's coats scratched along the meringue surface of the churchyard. John Dark Sky broke the coating of ice on one bale of hay Father slid off the wagon for the sheep.

Father broke the rest of the ice shield from the fly and untied the wagon flaps, chipping their icy gnarls loose with the butt of his knife. A smoky cooking fire soon brought coffee to a boil and Father produced the last of the boar's bacon and stirred spoonbread batter into a skillet with it.

Moses and I removed much of the icy sweater coating from the sheep and the mules and shook out the blankets that covered the horses. The animals shared the hay with the sheep and Father gave them the last of the oats we brought along with us. One sack of grain would have to do for them for the time being, much as we knew they would lose weight on that diet.

John Dark Sky was doing something to the wagon wheels besides chipping the ice from the spokes. He had winched one side of the wagon up a few inches off the ground using a tree limb and was wrapping the rims of the wheels on that side with leather straps cut from one of his deer hides. So we would be traveling this Monday morning. He returned the wagon to its four wheels and slid the sling along the axle to lift the other side and repeat the strapping of the wheels.

The result was thick tread for the wheel, a platform to keep the wheel from slipping off the icy path we were to travel.

A final wave to the minister and his wife and child and we crunched out of the churchyard and turned into the road, breaking through the crust of ice but not slipping as we went. At times that morning it became slow for the mules. The wagon wheels broke the ice where the snow was an inch or two deep, but for most of the bright wintry morning and afternoon we crunched lively along the hard crust.

When we stopped that afternoon in a small grove of maples, Father reckoned we had traveled nearly half the way to Dunkirk and the mules seemed none the worse for wear. The cold grew more intense and great breaths rose from the mules' mouths and noses, but the wind died down and we enjoyed reflections of silvery trees and sky in the mirror of ice all around us.

Silence settled in around us on the cold afternoon when we stopped for the day. A small creek, frozen into its serpentine shape, wound around the hillock we sat perched upon. The creek curved around us and fed into a frozen lagoon we crossed without realizing we had approached it. Or rather John Dark Sky knew that it was ice that would support our wagon wheels and that the sheep would not fear. Moses was soon chipping away at the lagoon ice with the maul.

I brought over a hatchet to help finish the hole he was breaking in the ice. He had a good idea, for I often caught fish through the ice along the shore of the Hudson River.

"Have you ever fished through the ice, Moses?" I asked, taking a turn with the maul.

"No, I think the fish might be hungry though. Do they freeze too sometimes?" he asked.

"I don't think we'll catch the frozen ones," I replied, handing the maul back to Moses and blowing on my cold had. "I am hungry for fresh fish."

Moses finished the hole, and it filled in with water as I brought the poles and unwound the lines. Moses attached salt pork to one hook and dropped his line down into the hole. The water was shallow but the inch of ice he cut through made it an overall depth of almost three feet of line he let out. In not two minutes he tugged a twelve inch perch up onto the ice. The fish flapped for a minute and quickly stiffening into and icy shape, its gills and fins spread wide.

In another minute, I caught a perch as big as the one Moses was gutting. Inside ten minutes, we had a supper of four perch and a large sunfish. I scooped the entrails together and dropped back in the hole, now slushy with ice.

Moses caught another perch before we wound the lines back onto the cards. The hole was already beginning to freeze into slush. If we awoke before dawn, a little fishing the next morning might provide us breakfast as well. And here was John Dark Sky with a partridge as well.

"I heard no rifle, John Dark Sky," I said. "Did you throw a stone to down it?"

"It flew up into a branch and brained itself," he said. Food seemed to be rising up to us, and falling around us like the snow.

We spitted the partridge and panfried the fish with salt pork and corn meal. It was sumptuous supper for being so far from Buffalo's wharves or Rochester and the canalboats with their ready supplies.I hoped we would have as much provision in the journey before us into new states.

In the morning, the ice had sealed our fishing hole, but we used the hatchet and in no time had the hole open again. Luck was with us once again, and we took six more perch to the pan for breakfast. Moses hooked a bigger fish, but he could not lift it to the surface before it broke the line. Our remaining hooks were too small to try again for that fish. The perch were more than enough for us four as well. We could make new hooks during turns on the wagon.

Towards noon, we struck Dunkirk, a few docks and a water tower on a railroad siding next to the main rail. For two days we had seen only one train pass, going west also. Two wagons, traveling on a westward route like ours, passed and the families chatted in friendly ways before they went on.

Lake Eerie had broadened so that we could not see across from Dunkirk, not even from the rounded tops of the sandy hills along the shore on this clear day. The sand was windswept into ten- and twenty-foot heights, dunes Father called them, and we were almost warm on the lee sides, out of the wind on this sunny day.

Our progress, slow as it was through the snow, was steady. Twelve miles, sometimes fifteen miles each day, seventy to eight miles each week. By Christmas, we hoped, we would be near to Ohio. This last stretch of New York was the most uninhabited and the most beautiful part of the state. As we caught glimpses of Lake Eire between the dunes, it was a silver platter with scalloped edges rolled onto a glasstop shore. Nearly every defile between the dunes was marked by a frozen inlet, a carving knife, a black blade of ice plunged between the snow-covered dunes. It was comic to see the sheep cautiously approach these inlets, a few bolder sheep started across, then the entire flock scampered across the ice, tripping up the far bank.

Our path skirted some of these inlets, crossed over others, reflecting the undercarriage and spokes where the wind had swept the ice dark, and then we climbed on along the base of another dune. The second evening, our protection was a fir forest growing up to the edge of the lake, a bank of pines with seed cones for kindling. John Dark Sky showed us the kernels inside certain cones and how to roast them for the best tasting nut, Moses said, since the goobers peas that grew in Louisiana.

It was snowing again the last day we would drive the sheep in New York State. We came upon a carriage abandoned on the side of the road with a broken axle. The wind played havoc on the carriage even though the leather roof was still intact. Its lantern had snapped off, and the isinglass on the passenger side was cracked, spider webbed with small pieces broken off inside the carriage. It had been a fine carriage, the kind a person of means might have owned. Moses asked if we could take the glass curtain that had been broken and Father said yes, that it would not be salvageable and the snow had already ruined the inside anyway.

We quickly carefully detached the curtain and folded it into layers, cracked as they were, between pieces of John Dark Sky's deerskins and paced them under other hides in the back of the wagon, wedged between the hay bales and the edge of the wagon. We left the abandoned wreck behind, glad that ours was in good condition and thankful to be coming soon to a more populated town: Erie, in Pennsylvania.

XVI

I DO NOT KNOW precisely at what point our wagon crossed into Pennsylvania. The land all looked the same, snow-covered sand dunes, frozen inlets forming the icy shoreline of Lake Erie. With no sign to release us from our long crossing of New York State, the moment was lost. For two days we had not seen a wagon or a rider. The shorebirds were our only neighbors as we drove the sheep along a windblown, snowpacked trail.

John Dark Sky rode back to us as evening came on. He pointed from the direction he had come and said, "Erie lies two miles on."

"Good news, Father said. "We'll seek shelter there tonight."

It was enough to inspire us to hurry, and even the sheep sensed an event just ahead. Or perhaps it was our ardor that Shep and the dogs passed on to the sheep.

We rode into Erie towards sunset. The docks had long since been shut for the day, this 23rd day of December. Barges were tied idle to long docks. A steamboat was tethered to one barge with its stack pluming, perhaps to keep the crew warm. Fishing boats, turned upside down on racks or covered with canvas, had collected ice and snow.

I wondered what kind of men would venture forth on Lake Erie in this season, to tow a barge loaded with timbers or coal or blocks of brownstone destined for some distant port on the lakes. But then, here we were, destined for a distant state, and this the time of year for families to be together to celebrate Jesus' birth. Here we were not even tied to a dock but drifting afar, but we were not following the guidance of a star, not seeking a king.

We found that the town of Erie was a cluster of houses and storage sheds, a port town, the northernmost town in a new state to which we had never traveled, or only Father had, and only southerly. Only briefly had I been in Massachusetts and once, in Connecticut. This was the fourth state for me.

For Moses, being in Pennsylvania was not exceptional. He had been in Mississippi, Louisiana, Tennessee; and Virginia and Maryland on his journey to Washington. And then, by railroad, from Washington through Delaware and New Jersey to New York. So for him, a new state, like others he had passed through, was nothing to celebrate.

But we would celebrate the next day. When we had arranged our campsite for the night, I mentioned the rush mats we had made. Father and John Dark Sky had gone to the docks to discover what ports lay along the southern shore of Lake Erie. Moses and I crept under the wagon to brush the snow from the undercarriage to retrieve our mats.

A few finishing touches – winding twine to whip the ends and finish the edges – and we were done. We admired the mats as if they were the finest of gifts from the Orient. Moses wanted to try them as sleds on the dune we had come to rest behind for the night.

"These are for Father and John Dark Sky, not for us," I reminded him. But I admit I too was eager to try sledding down the snowy dune. So we replaced the mats and ran up to the top of the dune and slid down on our bellies like otters, up again and down, wearing a smooth trough for next and faster slide.

We were still at our game when Father called that supper was ready. It was past dark, but a brightness from the rising moon and the firelight gave us light to see.

The steamboat crew had precious little food to spare, but Father traded whiskey for the small sturgeon they had netted, and so here was a feast again. Sturgeon, the fish we had come to be so fond of on the upper reaches of the Hudson, baked again, savory to the nose after our sliding contest. Father filled our plates and we drank hot tea to warm our insides. Pennsylvania was becoming a good place to celebrate a holiday even though we missed Esopus and wondered what Sarah and Ruthie would be doing this night before Christmas Eve.

I did not want to stop until the snow really set in. We had a full two hours of sunlight left to drive the sheep and we could put some distance between us and Erie and we would be that much farther on towards Wisconsin. But Father said we had to honor the events of the seasons. That we had to prepare ourselves for Christmas. But it wasn't a Sunday. Sunday had been only two days ago.

There was no changing Father on the subject of religion. Better to make the best of it and enjoy another break from sheep herding. "I'm going to see about a wreath," Moses said. I helped John Dark Sky herd the sheep into a paddock next to a livery across the road from the Presque Inn, a timbered, two-story establishment with smoke curling straight up out of two chimneys. Then I followed Moses' tracks back along the trail where we went through a snowy pine grove.

I found him cutting boughs. We each gathered armfuls of greens enough for six wreaths. Moses sorted the branches, and I stacked them by color, length of needles, and shape. Kentucky pine branches make the best base for wreaths, I discovered. We were going to have the "Santa Claus's sleigh" of Conestoga wagons, and we were going to do it in style. Wreaths on both sides, on the front of the wagon, and on the back too. On the mules' traces and on the wheels. Even the horses' bridles.

We clipped the branches and stripped off the unneeded twigs and pine cones. It was cold work. Bittersweet vines we tugged off on the smaller pine branches scratched my hands, but I couldn't feel much except the aching from the cold. We kept on working.

Taking time away from the wreath project, we warmed up in the Presque Inn. An hour later, we went back outside and wove the branches around the two spare wheels of our wagon as it stood in the inn yard. I added sprigs of holly and velvety red sumac and bittersweet berries clipped from our rope of vines. The wheels of the wagon began to lose their circular shapes under the nests of evergreens Moses twined around them and spun along their spokes and on up the sides of the wagon.

I tore strips from the red shirt I had outgrown and fashioned ribbons to go on the wreaths. Moses experimented with the isinglass we commandeered from the wrecked coach to see about an icy-like border, but it fell off when Father came out to move the wagon to the front of the inn across from the livery. He was duly impressed with our decorations, but his bumping back over the frozen ruts in the road detached the isinglass outlines of the wagon.

Moses helped John Dark Sky unhitch the mules and I unsaddled the horses and bedded them down in the livery. Then Moses and I went to put the finishing touches on the wagon.

Front and back of our wagon soon were bedecked like the sides, each with a wreath, and we bound the rest of the greens into pine ropes that we draped over the wagon stays. If we could have dyed the sheep red and green, we would have. But as it was, children's heads turned as a family rolled into the Presque Inn courtyard. They, like father, decided to stay as soon as they saw the inn. The road V-ed south and the lake road went straight, and it was clear enough and light enough for travelers to go on. But none did. Amazing to us, three other wagons stopped at the livery making altogether five families to be at the inn. As we finished draping the greens on our wagon, I told Moses, "Isn't it just like a pageant? Here we are shepherds and it's clear, getting to be a starry Christmas Eve. I expect a mother giving birth to a baby in the livery any minute."

"You can say all you want Jesse," Moses said, picking the snow out of his laces. "It is a good story and it's fine to see it relived. If I find a small kitten and put it in the livery, if there aren't already a few there, the cat and the kitten can be Mary and Jesus and it will be fine. Just fine. Just fine."

"Whatever did I say?" I asked him, astonished to see him so fit be tied. "I'm not putting a wet blanket on Christmas, Moses. You and I both decorated the wagon. I trimmed it up too."

"It's just that you always turn away from finding a purpose or a meaning or try to belittle the charm a place can hold."

"But you want to keep the driving the sheep Sundays too, just as much as I do, Moses. And you don't want to go into cold meeting houses for Quaker Meeting any more than I do."

"I'm beginning to see it your father's way," he said.

That was the first sign I had that this journey had thrown him. For Moses to admit that he felt Father was right about Sundays. That was desperation. He went on, "I guess I still do want to keep on, but here we are barely two weeks behind your uncle Peter. We've more'n made up a week and we took ten extra days of rest. Must be your father's right. Sundays are days for rest. Maybe he was right about other things too, like stopping here for Christmas Eve and Christmas Day. And reading the Bible evenings and saying grace over our meals and telling stories about Gideon, and King David and Saul, and Herod."

I looked at the wagon trimmed with the greens. We had both worn out our hands. I looked across to the livery where we had wisely bedded the horses and mules. The sky was clear, but who was to know? It might snow again. Maybe Father was right about stopping.

I looked over to the sheep in the livery paddock, munching their hay. The stars were brilliant in the sky and reflected out a ways past the peninsula, where Lake Erie hadn't frozen entirely. A trail of smoke went up into the air from Presque Inn's big fireplaces. It was silly. I almost began to feel that maybe Moses was right.

But then I remembered the Sermon on the Mount — about the meek inheriting the earth. Uncle Peter had been shunned by the so-called Christian neighbors in Esopus after he couldn't farm anymore. They blamed him for his incapacities. Wasn't he one of the meek? Weren't the meek plain people that needed stories and songs to take the place of what they couldn't find in their lives?

But stories like the birth of Jesus, they were just that — stories. "Stories are only stories, Moses, not rules for living or commandments from God."

"Stories are told with breath and breath is life, Jesse. You remember that. And when you write whatever it is you write in your journal, write it story-like sometimes. It is your story and it's my story. Because we are in it, it may not seem like it is a whole, or a plan, but it is. Even if it's only a part of a plan. It could be a piece of a bigger story, and so we'd do best to enjoy it for that."

"You tell it, Moses. You can tell you children about every inch of it."

"You can't see it?" he asked. "You don't understand yet that you are writing it down not because you want to but because you have to?"

"It's just about driving sheep," I tried to argue.

"It's about many more things than sheep."

We sat around the big fireplace in the Presque Inn with four other families after a supper of turkey and smoked venison. The stars were still bright and new snow was falling, but it was already a snowy Christmas because of accumulation in the past week. Moses was whittling a willow whistle and I was reading a book by Washington Irving that alternately put me near asleep and made me feel I was reliving the story. Except Washington Irving's Christmas traveler was going by coach and we were going by wagon and horseback.

John Dark Sky went outside to see whether one family's wagon wheel could be trued, or whether one of our spare wheels might be better for them, and then we would take theirs to be straightened.

I was listening to Father tell the innkeeper, Mr. Bailey, about our trip along the canal. Then Mr. Bailey told Father about the road to Cleveland. "Don't plan on the lake road being open all the way. There've been some storms that have covered the road along the shore and inland a ways."

"We'll follow the course set by my brother, who must have passed this way two weeks back with his sheep. But he didn't stop here?"

"I don't recollect anyone else with sheep. He may have come through during the worst part of the snow. But just because we didn't see him doesn't mean he turned south. He might have passed and not stopped."

"But Peter couldn't be missed by others. Not with his flock of sheep. Where might he have gone south to find better passage?"

"South along French Creek, possibly. Or Shenango River. Both are said to be frozen over though."

"Where from there, if he might be looking for better weather?"

"Both feed into the Allegheny River somewheres south of here. He might be bent for Pittsburgh, perhaps."

Father looked into the fire, thoughtful. John Dark Sky brought in a small bundle wrapped in a rabbit pelt. He set it down on the hearth and sat down on the hearth next to it.

Father stirred from his thought, then, and stood up. "Jesse, Moses, come over here. We have something for you."

It was to be Christmas, then, and tonight! I said, "Just a minute!" excitedly, and Moses and I ran outside to the wagon. We pulled the rush mats we had woven for Father and John Dark Sky out from under the flooring of the wagon and rolled them into bundles. Moses grabbed a wreath off the back of the wagon and ringed the mats with it as we walked back in, stomping our feet as we came onto the porch. "They'll be pleased with these. I'm glad we found the rushes and made good use of them."

"What do you think we're going to get?" Moses asked.

"It doesn't matter," I said. "It's a thoughtful thing, and I feel ever so much more like Christmas."

"Good," Moses said. "It always helps to have a present."

Good old Moses. He always gets a good lick in, even if it takes him awhile to think it up.

We reentered the cheery warmth of the main lodge and waited while Father finished talking with a few other men standing by the fireplace. John Dark Sky was explaining to one about the wheel we had traded him and about anchoring it with the dowel arrangement the man's wagon had.

Father was listening more than talking, I noticed. Listening and thinking. Then he looked into the fire and did the most unexpected thing I could imagine. He spat into the flames. It was a gesture that I hadn't seen before and haven't seen since.

Father straightened and lifted a poker to stir the fire. Sparks showered up into the chimney. "Be careful, there, Stiles, or you'll scare away Santy," said a big man to whom Father had been listening.

The men all laughed Father laughed too. He turned toward Moses and me and said, "Well, boys, it's time some Christmas came your way."

He nodded to John Dark Sky and John Dark Sky went into the room where we would be sleeping. When John Dark Sky returned to the main room of the lodge, he had a new red flannel shirt for each of us. "They're big enough so you won't outgrow them for a while." We traded bundles and Father looked surprised. Maybe he was really unsuspecting, but John Dark Sky looked enigmatic as ever, bowing slightly and smiling as he accepted his mat, but showing neither surprise nor emotion.

"Where did you find them?" I asked, surprised myself at not having noticed the shirts in the wagon, if that's where they had been.

"Back in Utica," Father said. "You were so involved with the town children that you wouldn't have noticed if I had shaved my beard. But see what John Dark Sky has done for you." He reached to lift the smaller bundle John Dark Sky brought in.

He handed us each a bone-handled knife. The blade was hand tempered and the bone handle bore carving that was unmistakably John Dark Sky's. The same firm hand that had drawn the map of our trip in hard earth in

Esopus had taken a sharp tool and with steady sureness etched a river and hills and treetops into the bone of each handle.

I was speechless. It was Moses who managed, "Thank you, John Dark Sky. This is a fine knife."

I could only hold the carving in my hands, turning it over and then slowly running the blade along the back of my hand, admiring the way it shaved the hairs off my wrist.

John Dark Sky smiled, showing his teeth. He rolled his mat up and turned toward the fire.

He did not know the Lake Erie land to draw maps like the map on the knife handle. His people could have been those that had come this way and farther west. But he could lead us along a Lake Erie shoreline. Or were we going south, to avoid the ice and snow? Even then, there would a trail and he could find it. There could be as much bad weather along the Allegheny River though. Maybe even worse weather, although we were west of the Allegheny Mountains now. The snow would not likely be as heavy.

It was Father who gave us the bad news in the morning, Christmas morning: "You boys and John Dark Sky will go along the lake to Cleveland. The weather may be worse, but Peter may turn back north to meet us.

"In the event that does not, I will find his route and proceed along it until I determine where he has gone. Then I will return to you, perhaps as early as Cleveland. More likely, a settlement the travelers call Sandusky."

After Father left the table, Moses said, "At least you will have your wish now. We can travel Sundays too."

Father reentered the dining room and announced, "You, Jesse, will see to it that the day of the Lord is observed. Jesse?"

"Yes, sir." I smirked at Moses.

XVII

Father and John Dark Sky were up before daylight the next morning, December 25. Snow was falling again. Father placed a saddle blanket over Boca's haunches and his rifle in its sling next to the saddle. He loaded saddlebags and lifted them onto Boca. The horse had brought him a long way from the war. Where would Boca take him now? John Dark Sky was talking softly to Boca and stroking his ears. Father tightened the cinch and swung up onto the saddle. It was Christmas Day and there was Father, ready to depart.

I hadn't thought about Mother much lately, but for some reason her face was in my thoughts. Maybe it was the face in the portrait over her bureau. It was her face though.

Father turned Boca halfway around and leaned down to knock the snow from his stirrup. Moses stood beside me. He was whittling with his new knife.

Father took a small clothwrapped package out of his coat and handed it to John Dark Sky. "Carry this," he said, "in case it might be needed." He looked out past us. "Goodbye, Moses. Goodbye, Jesse. Help John Dark Sky with the sheep."

"We will," Moses asserted.

I nodded. There was no word I could say that would help at this moment. No word for Father nor for me, to help me. I could only raise my hand. That was all I had by way of farewell for Father.

We had been together less than one short year since the war. How long would it be before I would see him again? "Cleveland," he had said, "or Sandusky." Or perhaps it would be father on. Toledo. Chicago. Places

I never imagined. Wisconsin. And why were we going there? Why was it important to go? Was it the drought? Was it to save Uncle Peter? Was it to fulfill a promise Father had made to a wounded officer? Or was it to go, simply and undeniably to the west, south, anywhere?

Father turned Boca into the road and plodded off through the new snow, a scarf tied around his hat, covering his head and neck. The saddle blanket was spread over Boca's flanks. Fastened to the back of Father's saddle was a roll of reeds. Our mat. Seeing the mat there, on Boca's back, flooded my eyes with tears. I quickly wiped my eyes so no one would see. When I looked up again, Boca's tail was fluttering in the falling snow like a flag. It was an adventure for him, but I wished the adventure to be over, to be caught up with Uncle Peter and setting the sheep out to pasture somewhere in Wisconsin, not floundering in the snow here in Pennsylvania.

Moses touched my sleeve. "Come up to the paddock. We've time to make a snowman before breakfast." The day was just beginning to turn gray over the lake. Father left before breakfast; we were to leave as soon after the meal as we could and still be gracious guests. A snowman wouldn't hurt. I could accept that distraction. Good old Moses.

The Baileys had prepared the waffle batter the night before. The sponge rose slowly all night, pressed down sometime early, before Father awoke, just as Sarah had made it so many times. Moses bounded into the inn's reception hall through a kitchen door to report the feast. The aroma of waffles followed him and seemed to sweep into the dining room and mingle with the smell of porridge cooking over the hearth. John Dark Sky ladled porridge into a wooden bowl and toed a big log in the fireplace a quarter turn.

Distraught as I felt about Father's leaving, my appetite was keen. "This is the last meal where we'll be warm inside and out," Moses said. He scooped a ladleful of porridge into a bowl and poured sorghum over it. I took a bowl and ladled it half full, then added another portion and two dips of the thick, dark syrup.

Mr. Bailey brought a platter loaded with waffles. "The first of many-a-waffle-iron-full," he called to the family whose children were looking wide-eyed at the Christmas tree. Mr. Bailey set the steaming platter on the sideboard next to the tree. "Breakfast first," he said to the children; then you may each help yourself to a present."

I wondered if he was referring to Moses and me too, if we were thought of as children, and I decided we were not. Father had left us, and so we were adults. The empty feeling inside began to be replaced with the thought of being adult.

We ate till we were certain there would be no waffles left, when out of the kitchen yet again came a tray of those fluffy waffles and what looked like a basket of biscuits, this time brought by Mrs. Bailey doing up a loosened strand of her hair and smiling on the assembly. "Mr. Bailey and I are so glad you have joined our Christmas celebration this year," she sang out.

She came up next to Moses and put her hand on his shoulder. He gave her his enormous smile and stood for her to sit on the bench. She did sit and glanced behind her at the sideboard still encumbered with waffles and serving dishes pile high with biscuits and jellies and cream.

Other guests were still partaking of the breakfast feast, but Moses and I thanked Mrs. Bailey and excused ourselves.

"You must come back on your return, boys," Mrs. Bailey said, extending her hand. I took her hand, warm and strong, in mine, and then Moses took her hand and bowed.

"We surely will be back," he said. "Whenever that may be."

John Dark Sky had finished his meal and was stomping his feet on the porch as we walked outside. He lifted a basket of provisions the Baileys put up for us and pointed with it to the wagon. "We will leave soon," he said. "The sheep are ready on the road."

The snow stopped, leaving only a light dust on the porch rails and the road and adding a frosting to the white landscape. John Dark Sky stepped off the inn's porch and took his horse's reins. Moses looked back at the glow from inside the Presque Inn, took a deep breath and pulled his hat down over his forehead. I went with him down the steps of the inn and across to the livery. I would drive the wagon first and Moses would spell John Dark Sky. Then I would ride and John Dark Sky would sit the wagon. The snow would restrict the wandering of the sheep and so only one rider needed to travel horseback with them. We could use both mules to pull the wagon and one of us could rest or drive.

I found the mules already hitched to the wagon and stomping in the gray snow. Snow was mixed with straw outside the livery. The greens around the wheels were removed, by John Dark Sky most likely. To allow freer tracks through the snow, I suspected. I climbed to the driver's seat while Moses took one last look at our snowman and then hopped up beside me. The mules ambled out of the inn road and onto the icy lake road, trampled down by the sheep in the snowscape ahead of us.

A sunrise somewhere behind us was turning the lake silver and winking off the fields alongside us, making it hard to see the sheep.

"I'm not ever sure the sheep are up there with all this brightness," Moses said.

"There're up there all right," I said, "else we wouldn't have this well-worn road under our wheels."

"Where are we going to feed them today?" Moses asked, a concern that plagued me as well.

"We'll find a place. This snow is only up to the lake. There are many places along the railroad from now on too, and we have all the hay yet in the wagon." I wondered what distances passed between the stops on the railroad and whether we might be forced to turn south, like Uncle Peter. And whether Father would find Uncle Peter and Cotton. And us. "We'll be fine, Moses." But I wondered.

Somewhere as the sun slipped into the graying sky, Moses replaced John Dark Sky in the saddle. John Dark Sky took the wagon reins from me. I lay on the hay inside the wagon. It was getting colder and we would soon have to find rest for the night, but John Dark Sky wanted to go on. It was not so much that we had to make any great distance before night. John Dark Sky had a sense about better shelter or coming across another family on the road for company or taking advantage of a clear road while there was still a clear road to be traveled.

The icy road made for slow bumping along. My hat slipped over my eyes. My feet grew cold in the wagon. I stuffed my feet between two bales of hay and wondered if Father had found shelter and if he was cold as well.

Chances were he had located a place out of the wind, if not for himself, then for Boca. And he would want us to stop for the night. We ought to. He would have said to.

He would stop because he and Boca must be strong to catch up with Uncle Peter. Only now it was not just the sheep. It was to be until Cleveland or Sandusky or Toledo when Boca returned Father to us. They would expect us to be along the way. To keep the sheep along the way.

And we must be strong to keep the sheep underway. In a dream, Father was saying to stop. The wagon bumped over a frozen rut and stopped. I looked out the blanket that covered the front of the wagon and saw a dark tent of pine before us. Moses gathered sticks to make a fire over near the sheep gathering under the trees. The sheep were scratching at the pine needles. I stretched and pulled my hat straight. The bale I had loosened for comfort and warmth was still partly bound and I toed it off from the wagon. I hopped off and spread some of the loose hay from the end of the bale over the soft snow for the sheep. Moses looked up from the fire he was blowing to start as it began to catch and snap. He came to the wagon to fetch the coffeepot. We hadn't said more than two sentences since we stopped. John Dark Sky took his rifle and disappeared.

So this was our shelter. Two dozen pines arranged against a hillside covered with snow. I pulled down the blanket from the front of the wagon and shook the loose hay from its wool weave. Stepping back down from the wagon, I wrapped the blanket around my shoulders and joined Moses by the fire. The flame was turning yellow and the wood spit and steamed.

Somewhere over the hill John Dark Sky's gun popped. "There's our rabbit," I said. "Let's hope it'll be something we can clean quickly."

"I'm not tired yet of deer meat," Moses said. "I'll eat it if it's a deer and if you'll gut it out."

"Your generosity is as big as you," I said, and he laughed.

The fire flared up and settled. Moses placed a bigger pine branch across the flames.

The small white snowshoe rabbit, hard enough to see in its summer coat, was skinned and sizzling on a spit. It was our supper, it and the coffee with no sheep's milk because the ewes were not giving enough milk to suckle the lambs as it was. They fared better in this weather if they were not suckling, and we had fewer problems when the sheep were not milked. I thought of Sarah and wondered if she was well, whether the winter was harsh in Esopus, and how big Ruthie must now be.

"Moses, you haven't even seen your little sister since she was no bigger than the rabbits John Dark Sky finds. She'll be grown up by the time we get back."

"I imagine Mother is telling her all about us, Jesse. We shall spoil her when we get back we'll be giving her so much attention."

John Dark Sky shifted the hay in the wagon and scattered my hay on the ground for his horse and for the sheep. We would all sleep in the wagon tonight. Father would sleep where he could. He would find shelter. And warmer weather, as he went.

XVIII

Daylight only intensified the cold until we set the fire ablaze. Why did I tear off my clothes and run into the small creek that ran under the bridge where we pitched our camp, and dip my body once in the spring that had melted the surface ice, splash the black water into my face, then race back to the fire and dance into my clothes again, my feet and legs afire with the cold? Moses shook his head and poured me a hot cup of coffee. John Dark Sky set my boots near the fire to warm them so my feet would thaw faster.

I hooted and blew into my coffee every few seconds to fill my face with the warm steam. The fire was melting snow in a gray arc. I began to feel warm even though I had not pulled my boots on yet.

"Get your boots on or you'll lose a few toes," Moses advised.

"It's greatly refreshing," I said, my teeth still chattering. "I feel warm. Try a bath yourself."

"Not if the dogs won't," Moses said, looking at Shep and the other dogs nose the water at the spring's edge.

We spent an hour repacking the wagon until, filling the morning with golden light. Sunlight broke through the cloudbank to the east.

"The day will be good," John Dark Sky said. He was forking some of the untouched hay up into the wagon and restacking deerskins that loosened. Then, I don't know why, he kicked snow over the remains of our fire, and we left our pine grove and followed the sheep west again.

On the road to Cleveland that morning, the sheep plodded steadily ahead. But they went more and more slowly until we were making only a mile or so every hour. We couldn't make such distance, five miles, and call a halt. We wouldn't make Cleveland by February at that rate. But John Dark Sky left it up to the sheep. "They are wise in their ways," he said, more than once, when I complained about their pace.

All that day and all the next two days, the sheep followed the road as if in a trance. We spent nights in the wagon, shivering in our clothes under John Dark Sky's deerskins and blankets. At least it had not snowed since the day we left the Presque Inn. John Dark Sky would fold a blanket around himself twice and lean against the stay that held our fly against the wind. I rarely saw him asleep. He was up and after fowl or rabbits mornings before either Moses or I arose.

Inside a week's march to Cleveland, we junctioned with a road that seemed to come up from the south. John Dark Sky studied the marks of the horses that had turned along that road, trampling the packed snow in our direction of travel. The marks were clear enough to tell how many riders there had been, six or seven. The only other signs were wagon ruts several days old. Our own wagon was making slower progress than ever.

Then there were fewer farms, almost none together in settlements on the road to Cleveland. Travelers on this desolate stretch were horseback or afoot. No wagons passed going east. One matter puzzled us though, and it made John Dark Sky quieter than he already was: signs of trails going off into the woods at odd junctions, off to the north, towards the railroad or Lake Erie. As if something drew the travelers off the trail or sent them scurrying. And why were the marks brushed over at times, as if to hide where they had left the trail? And why were there only cloth or leather wrappings where boots should have been? Were these people poor, hurrying off the road, trying to avoid being followed?

I wanted to take one of those concealed trails to its end to see who these people were, where they were going, but we were committed to going on west. The trails bothered both Moses and me more each time we found them.

"I know that kind of leaving of the road," Moses remembered. "When the Southern troops came back, whole families would light out off the roads from the main houses where they had been staying, waiting. They'd make for the bayous to wait to see whether their former masters would receive them. One or two would make their way back to test the water, to see if they would be welcome.

"Sometimes it was only the livestock that would be welcomed back into the main house. Horses on the porch and walking right into the kitchens out back. But few former household servants.

"And then if they were not welcome, families would move on. Some came to our island. Others stayed and rebuilt their old slave quarters, to be servants again for their old master, except they couldn't be slaves then. They mostly didn't have their masters to help them."

"They were still providing, but they weren't provided for."

"Mostly, yes," Moses said.

"What did Father do when he learned about such?" I wondered.

"I never heard," Moses said. "What could he do that he hadn't already tried to do to make it work?"

"I don't know. I wasn't there. He would have done something though."

But if these trails, secret forays away from the road to Cleveland, were the paths of poor Negroes migrating from Southern settlements, why were they frightened? Who was after them?

"They are a freed people, aren't they?" I asked Moses.

"They surely don't act like it, if they are," Moses said, looking off ahead.

I was beginning to be concerned about something other than Father, something I couldn't put words to. Who were the horsemen, following the ragged trails, worrying the migrating people off the road, sending them into a wilderness of uncharted woods?

I said it to John Dark Sky, "Something is wrong."

"Not good," was all John Dark Sky suggested.

We settled along the road for the night near one of the side trails leading off north around a sandy, snow-covered berm that afforded protection from winds coming off Lake Erie. All that night, the wind blew against the wagon, and in the morning, the sheep were caked with a dusty snow coating. The wagon was festooned with snow on the north-facing side, wheels nearly spokeless with the wall of blown sandy snow.

We dug out of the drift we had created with our wagon windbreak, and the mules plowed us onto the main road, the sheep coming along behind us.

Blowing drifts covered the road, and we saw no more of the side trails. Maybe the wind covered them over where they had not before been brushed. Maybe ours was the last side trail.

Just into the town of Painsville, the trailed joined with a well-marked road off to the south. A carved sign pointed to a place called Akron. We came to a river or inlet off the lake that we could not ford. Low as it was, we weren't about to risk getting the wagon stuck in the middle of freezing water if the ice broke under us.

John Dark Sky took just south along the river. It joined a larger river and we followed that river farther south. We later heard it called the Cuyahaga River. We found the narrowest section of the river was where we had been, north near Lake Erie. The weather was better when we stopped for the night at a bend in the Cuyahaga River. I hoped we were still south on the main road to Akron. There was enough traffic indicated in wheel ruts, and runner paths also marked sledge traffic that came across country to this road.

The next morning, before I roused Moses, John Dark Sky was up and already gone. He had left a fire going strong to cook our coffee and warm the leftover stew we had only half-finished the night before, squirrel stew browned with the last of our salt pork from the boar. Moses woke up as I was repacking my bedding, and he and I ate it hungrily in the gray morning light.

Moses was tying down the flaps of the wagon as John Dark Sky rode in. "Some settlers spoke of Peter and Cotton," he said. "They are with soldiers. They might be on the road to the Ohio River. It is open water. The river can take all cargo. A flatboat can take the sheep."

Moses and I looked at each other. "But the opposite shore below Cincinnati is a slave state," I said. "Cotton should not travel on the Ohio River." I remembered what the Friends spoke about at school. Kentucky. And western Virginia. Still unsafe for any Southern Negro. Moses knew it too.

John Dark Sky looked down the road. Something about his look changed. Only for a moment, then he slid down off his horse and reached for the ladle still in the pot of stew. He brought a leather pouch from his saddle and filled it with the warm stew. He ladled four helpings of the gravy and few chunks of squirrel each in the snow for the dogs and left the pot for Shep to finish. He quietly ate and I cleaned the pot after Shep and wiped it dry with a leather cloth and packed the pot in the back of the wagon.

None of us mentioned the danger we felt lurking for Uncle Peter and Cotton. They must be safe, and yet we were uneasy.

We left, traveling south, we hoped on the Akron road, along the river we hoped was still the Cuyahaga.

XIX

SETTLER CABINS AND the foundation of one house dotted either side of the river road. Several 20 by 30-foot structures on stone pilings reminded me of similar cabins along the Mohawk River near Rochester, one-story stone houses with small windows, some with glass, some with parchment or with no coverings.

Moses was riding in the back of the wagon until he hopped down next to John Dark Sky, who was walking his horse, and fell in step beside a Negro pulling a sled with a layer of stones. John Dark Sky spoke to the man as I drove past on to the settlement and came upon a log house with blankets over the windows. In back of the house a tall Negro woman was drawing water at a well. She turned to survey the flock's passing. Moses waved. The woman raised her hand.

A child six or seven years old came out across the stone cabin step to a vantage point near the roadbed to try to touch the passing sheep. Moses hopped off the wagon again and carried a yearling lamb to the step so the child could pat it.

The woman came around to the step and set the pail of water on the stone. Moses tipped his hat brim as he had seen father and Uncle Peter and Cotton do so often. He spoke to the woman. She said something in reply to Moses. He nodded. Then Moses set the lamb down next to her child and motioned to me to come over to where they stood.

I turned the mules off to the side of the road so the flock of sheep could go on past with John Dark Sky. I got down and trudged across the snowy roadway to the small gathering on the step.

"How do you do," I greeted the woman.

"Howd'ya do," she replied. "This young man here said to tell you."

"Tell me what?" I inquired.

"The others. With the sheep. They gone by here last week."

"Uncle Peter! Only a week behind! Moses, we are nearly up to Uncle Peter."

"You can tell him," Moses said to the woman.

The woman took her child by the hand. "The soldiers with them. They are bad soldiers."

I looked at Moses. He looked down at the child.

The woman went on. "They are varmints." She spoke, spitting out the words.

A cold shiver went through me. Moses kept looking down.

"They sell us back. First, they take money to get us over here to freedom. Then they come back to get us and take us down to Kentucky for ransom."

"What kind of soldiers would do that? Not Union soldiers. Moses, there must be a mistake."

"No mistake," Moses muttered. "John Dark Sky knows. The man with the sledge told him."

"And he told you. And you didn't tell me?" I was at my wits' end.

"I wasn't sure. I overheard them talking back on the road. It still could be they're just going to take the sheep."

"And that's why we didn't cross the river to go to Cleveland." It came to me all at once. "John Dark Sky knew from the horses."

"That. And those other trails we saw, I reckon," Moses added.

John Dark Sky fanned out the flock where the settler woman's back lot was strewn with hay. Uncle Peter and Cotton must have stopped here the week before.

"Cotton!" I almost shouted to Moses. "He isn't safe!" I did shout this time.

"You 'alluns come in for a bite," the woman smiled, for the first time. "And the other gentleman come in too." She turned without waiting for an answer, picked up the pail, and stepped into the cabin, leaving the door ajar.

"Moses, we have to help Cotton."

"Cotton and Uncle Peter. He must be in trouble too. But how can we fight the soldiers?" He shook his head.

"We have to think of something. Give them all the sheep. Something." I was frantic.

John Dark Sky was suddenly at our side. "Go in," he said, and he stepped up into the cabin. I followed wondering how he knew we were asked in. Moses came after me.

The inside was well lit by a kerosene lamp, and a fire was heating a kettle of stew in the fireplace.

Three men were sitting on a bench at a table. We exchanged greetings. One, in furs, stood up to give me a seat. John Dark Sky stood next to him. Moses sat on an upended nail keg next to the fireplace.

"We talked to your man and the one with the missing hand," the one in furs said, "and told them. They didn't know until they stopped here."

"What will they do?" I asked.

"What will your men do, or what will the soldiers do?" another of the men asked.

"What will Uncle Peter do?"

"He wouldn't do much even if he had both his hands," the one with furs said. "Neither the other."

"What will the soldiers do?" I was afraid to ask but I had to.

"They take us all folk they can boat down the river to Lexington. To the slave traders."

Hot tears flowed out of the corners of my eyes into my mouth. I couldn't help myself. Moses bent over as if he had a cramp.

"We'll not let that happen," the one in furs said.

"But how? What can be done?" I asked. "How will you stop them?"

"We couldn't stop them. You can, though," he said. "We can help you."

The three men did not go with us. Neither did our sheep. We left the sheep to pasture and Shep and the dogs to guard them. The wagon sat in the same field and we took the mules. John Dark Sky rode his horse, I rode one mule, and Moses rode the other, to the Ohio River.

With every cabin we passed, every farm that Negroes were working, and at the small Akron Meeting House where we stopped on Sunday, we were keenly aware of companions, allied to our quest. Word of our coming traveled ahead of us.

We had food and lodging, not in barns but in cabins, sometimes on the floor but mostly wrapped in shawls and blankets on pallets of straw ticking near the warmth of chimneys.

In four days of traveling along the Tuscarawas River, we made Zanesville. The weather was much warmer and the road was clayey. Without the sheep we kept up a better pace. Worry kept us from tiring.

Along the Muskingham River from Zanesville another five days, we struck Marietta. Now the mules were thin from the miles. Moses was tired too, and sick from worry. Cotton was the father he accepted. And now Cotton was in grave danger.

Since Zanesville, we had seen no Negroes traveling the roads. No Negroes came to their doors to wave. Their cabins were noted by a lack of fencing or by missing panes of glass in windows. Or no windows, only doors opened a crack.

Our signal was a blanket hanging on the branch of a tree. Whenever that was noticed from the road, we could gain word of Cotton and Uncle Peter. It was sent out along our way as if by heralds.

Right before Marietta, a very old Negro woman with white hair told us to wait for word before proceeding to the Ohio River. That the boats were leaving in two days.

We had to set our plan in motion before the next day was upon us.

XX

THE SWIRLING WATER of the Ohio River: brown silt, debris from decks washed away by winter flood stage, a side wheel paddle steamer, surrounded in its own smoke, working its way upstream, a flock of Canada geese making a racket flying overhead. We were one day downriver from Marietta. Moses and I sat on the island, really a spit of land jutting from the shore, submerged where it joined the northern bank. Wakes from boat traffic washed over the shoreline where we sat. We could not see John Dark Sky or the others around the bend, waiting at Portsmouth's landing.

Uncle Peter's sheep were already bound for Western Virginia, sold, we learned. The wagon too was sold in Marietta, and Uncle Peter was in the town jail. The old woman brought us the news. Uncle Peter was accused of kidnapping Cotton. The so-called soldiers, they were the ones who had taken Cotton. And now Cotton was on the steamboat heading for Portsmouth landing, with four of those varmint bounty-hunting soldiers, and Uncle Peter in jail. The steamboat embarked from Marietta and would stop here in Portsmouth before heading downriver.

If John Dark Sky could steal Cotton back when the steamer was tied at the landing, we could go backcountry, avoiding the varmints. With the Negroes' help, we could retrieve Cotton and work our way back up the rivers to our remaining sheep.

"But what will we do about Uncle Peter?" I asked the old woman. "He may be sent to some other jail, maybe not even in Ohio."

"Your father is on his way. He will not be long. Our people will see to it that he is directed to Peter."

"How could a band of varmints like that kidnap people?"

"They are Morgan's Raiders," she told us," escaped from prison up in Columbiana County, and they are thieves. They stole four Northern uniforms. Since then, they have twice raided settlements and carried off our people down the river for illegal bounty."

The shrill whistle of the steamer sent a sick feeling to my stomach. It was just opposite us as it nosed into the bend where the water was quieter to slow for the landing. We could have jumped onto its deck from where we lay.

Moses and I heard the steamer whistle again twice; then we crossed the water and crawled through bushes across the sandy spit to watch the boat unloading.

When half the passengers were on the dock and the others already on the gang, three men in soldiers' uniforms left Cotton on the deck under the guard of a fourth man in uniform. Cotton's feet were tied. His hands were bound to his waist.

We waited what seemed like an hour, watching Negroes load pallets of goods into the steamer's bay, and some bags and containers from inside the steamer's bay were hoisted onto the dock and onto waiting wagons.

More Negroes loaded foodstuffs into the cook's deck on the river side of the steamer. Some of them milled about the cook's deck smoking and waiting for the containers to be emptied. Two went above to the deck where Cotton was bound. Next to where Cotton was bound.

Suddenly, Cotton was running and the man in uniform guarding him was shielded from Cotton by the two Negroes. The man in uniform slid to the deck, gently held against his fall by the taller of the two Negroes. The Negroes then went below deck to remove the now empty containers. Empty all but one. And return them to the landing.

The other three uniformed men returned smoking and passing a bottle from one to the next. They had not yet gone above.

We held our breath.

The emptied containers were being loaded onto wagons and pushed up the loading ramp to be hitched to teams.

A shot sounded just as the steamer cast off. Hands on deck released the lines quickly. The ship was not yet under full steam, but the strong current took it slowly away from the dock, just enough so the man in uniform running toward the half-raised ramp could not jump the last six feet to shore without injury or a bath in the frigid water. He fired his rifle once again, but the shot went harmlessly wild.

The containers were slowly hitched to wagons and the teams began to haul them up the road as the steamboat disappeared into the afternoon sun.

John Dark Sky and Cotton watched as the Negro drew a map on the shirting material with a stick of charcoal. We would have to go cross-country, through marshland we hoped was still frozen, and come from the west into the Lesters' farm, where we had left our sheep. It was a ten-day trip, but it would take us eleven or twelve going nights, even with clear weather and solid footing. I removed my compass from its sheath. It would be needed for much of this trip. I grasped the carved knife, John Dark Sky's present.

With the shirt map carefully folded into his saddlebag, John Dark Sky and I rode double on his horse and Cotton and Moses each rode a mule. We took one last look at the Negro mapmaker. He nodded once, then disappeared into the brushy margin of the river. We rode along the riverbank, eastward, for a spell, then knifed up a steep rise through dense pine growth.

Through the evening and into the night, we rode steadily, not stopping to build a fire, chewing on jerky and scooping up snow in our hands. Any other time I might have fallen asleep against John Dark Sky's back as the horse ambled over the moonlit fields. Tonight, I was on the lookout for any voices or sounds of horses, my every sense alerted.

A waxing moon cast eerie light on the snow as we crossed a farmer's pasture, and there was the telltale blanket on a branch near the gate.

Cotton slid off the mule and softly rapped on the back door. After a minute it opened a crack and then all the way. We were given blankets for the animals and soon the fire in the woodstove was crackling.

My hands burned as they warmed up, holding onto a hot mug of chicory that had real cream spooned into it. Moses curled up next to the hearth. The stout woman who had opened for us bustled about in the cupboard, producing bread and preserves and butter on a cutting board.

It was a bigger house on the inside than it had seemed, partly dug as it was into the hillside. It was also smoky inside, but warm. The woman was whiter than Moses, almost as white as Mother's face was. The man was Negro, dark skinned like Cotton. A book of George Fox's writings was sitting on the dining room table with other books. They were Quakers, then. Like Father. Like me, as I was fast becoming, I realized.

"Many families you will meet are Friends," the woman explained. She produced thick slices of bread that we spread with the jams and butter on pottery plates. Each of us partook except Moses. He was fast asleep for the first time in three days.

Then the rest of us slept through the sunup till noontime and spent the afternoon inside, waiting for dusk. I went to the barn to help feed a hog and to gather eggs, but Moses, Cotton and John Dark Sky stayed within the house.

I hadn't had time to think about Uncle Peter, but when I came back from the barn, I suddenly wondered if he was all right. I asked Cotton, "Do you think we can go on with Uncle Peter?"

"He's safe in the jail" Cotton reassured me. "He may be uncomfortable, and he's probably upset with himself for trusting those varmints. But he won't run into harm there. When the town finds out that the soldiers were Southern, they will release Peter."

"But how will he find us?" I wondered.

"The same way you found me," Cotton reassured me. "If he doesn't already know where we are."

We prayed a long time before the evening meal, which was, for the first time on our trip, mutton. Then, after Moses and I cleared the plates, John Dark Sky spread the shirt cloth map out on the table. The husband pointed to hills that skirted their farm, how to get over them and how to stay away from the road. And how to find the bridge. We would have to cross the west branch of the Muskingham River, and there was but one bridge.

All that night, all the next night, and third night, and five more, we crossed frozen marshland, streams that were only open in the center a trickle. The eleventh night, we entered a road that led to the field and the house where had first learned about Uncle Peter and Cotton. Cotton recognized it right off. And there were our sheep. Shep raised a howl when he recognized us. And the other dogs came running and licking us too.

And then I saw a horse, unmistakable, Boca. And Uncle Peter's wagon. Father! Father was here! And Uncle Peter! And standing in the doorway, Father. And into his strong arms, burying my face now level with his into his bushy beard. Moses flung himself at Father next and we were being hugged by Father with his arms lifting us off our feet onto the stone step.

Behind him, standing in the glow of the fire, next to the Lesters, Uncle Peter was smiling.

XXI

"We wondered when you would arrive," Father said, hugging me and Moses both. Then he took Cotton's hand and, looking him in the eye as only Father can said, "Those must have been unhappy days for you, my friend. I don't know how to apologize for those men in uniform. If it's any consolation, they were not Union soldiers."

"How do you know that?" Cotton asked. "Peter, they were the First Ohio Brigade, were they not?"

Father looked at John Dark Sky. "You may have known, or you might have suspicioned, John," Father left off hugging us and stepped inside the Lesters' house to allow us to enter.

John Dark Sky said nothing, looking directly at Father.

"Their mount," Father said, looking past John Dark Sky to Uncle Peter. "Not shod in regulation, correct?"

John Dark Sky looked directly at Father.

"You knew, and that is how you knew you could intercept them, and trick them, and not endanger Peter or Cotton. Or only risk not retrieving Cotton wherever it was you did retrieve him until farther along at the next landing. Maybe not retrieving him until Cincinnati.

"Or worse," Uncle Peter added. "Kentucky or Missouri."

John Dark Sky smiled, as I had seen him smile only once since we set off on the twisting, turning journey of the last weeks, and that was at Christmas at the Presque Inn when Moses and I gave him his rush mat. And now here he was smiling again in the warmth of the Lesters' firelight. "And that is why," Father continued, "you took the boys with you. Because you knew the men held no authority over you or the boys." He looked at the Lesters.

Then Father turned and looked at Cotton. Cotton said, "They are no longer boys, John. They are not boys. They are ready to be men."

The Lesters were staring at us, standing in the center of the room with the morning light graying in the sky. "Please let us fix you some grits and eggs, some ham," said Mrs. Lester.

"We'd be obliged, yes," said Cotton. "You took a great risk in providing for us," he said to Mrs. Lester. "I know, and I thank you both."

"No risk involved," said Mr. Lester. "A risk would have been to do nothing. He took a copper kettle from the Franklin stove and poured cups of the steaming chicory for each of us. "You only needed these boys," he said, handing Moses a cup. "Men," he corrected himself.

"Only them. Yes," Cotton agreed.

Mr. Lester handed John Dark Sky a cup.

We sat down around the fireplace. John Dark Sky leaned against the chimney.

"How did you find Uncle Peter?" I asked Father.

"It was not so much finding him," Father replied. "It was waiting until Cotton was out of harm's way."

"The soldiers, if you wish to call them that, were Rebels. Escaped from prison camp," Father said. "Word of their escape and their disguise as Union soldiers and their chasing and kidnapping of freed families was on the lips of every Negro and a considerable number of whites. At one crossing, I was detained myself and had to go to Steubenville to telegraph Washington to confirm who I was. That I wasn't one of the varmints.

"And then word came of their travel with a flock of sheep and two men with them. But I didn't know about you and Jesse and Moses," Father said as he turned to John Dark Sky. Did you know my whereabouts?" he kept looking at John Dark Sky, adding, "until I arrived in Marietta? And that I would release Peter from jail? And that I would know I would not need to go for Cotton? That you already had?"

"In Marietta we heard about you. But about us, which person told you then?" I asked.

"The constable himself knew," Father said. "His servant knew and told him. And the constable told me. But they could not let Peter out for fear of risking Cotton's being taken directly across the river with the sheep."

"And so you couldn't risk it either, sir," Moses said, and suddenly Moses and I knew together. That Father taken no action because he knew a plan would have been set in motion. By the Negroes who were the landing workers and settlers, and, all along the river if necessary, with those who had word of John Hunt Morgan's Raiders. Because he, Father, knew that Cotton would be safe. And we would be safe. That to act himself, Father would risk interfering with a plan that would have been prepared, ordained even, by Negroes who would not allow its failure.

"So we lost Peter's sheep. But here we are," said Father, sipping his chicory. "Let us give thanks to the Lord."

We talked until noon, when Father insisted that we help the Lesters with the farm chores. He did not let us rest, but offered our help in forking out the hay for the sheep while he and John Dark Sky helped with the plowing and planting of the early crops, with Uncle Peter leading the mules. Other families, including those of the three men we had first met at the Lesters came to help and brought food that everyone shared for dinner.

A bright sun glinted off the fields and melted a good amount of the new cover, exposing the earth to its warmth and making us even drowsier. Moses and I finished with the sheep and went on feeding the chickens and cleaning the horses' hooves. We brushed Boca and John Dark Sky's horses until they shone. After the chores, we went into the warm house and collapsed on our pallets, sleeping soundly until the others trooped in from the fields. Supper was cooking over the coals in the fireplace and on the stove, and again, sleep overcame Moses and soon afterwards, me, and we pulled our pallets over to a corner and let the others walk to and from the fireplace where the kettle simmered with the beef stew, its aroma wafting into my sleep. The kettle would be simmering still when I awoke, and the quiet voices and clicking of knives became part of my dream.

I awoke once to see Father put another chunk of wood on the fire and poke its embers into a flame.

"You boys have some supper," he said.

"No thank you, sir," said Moses. He was awake too. We both fell asleep again and woke to Hannah Lester in her apron serving portions of stew in bowls on a platter.

"You boys need a little leftover supper?" she asked, prompting us to sit up.

I rose up on one elbow and accepted a plate and a cup of sheep's milk. Moses was already sitting up, his blanket wrapped around him. He helped himself to the bowl she offered. We each kneeled with our steaming bowls and dug into the tangy goodness.

Father opened the back door scraping mud and snow off his boots on the iron grid by the door. It was already full day and we had slept close to twelve hours. "You men up already?" Father asked, smiling.

But we knew we had been allowed. Even though we were now considered men after what we had been through. That we had been allowed, but we were expected now to get ready to go to battle. Luckily, it was not combat, but battle with the cold and frigid rivers and ceaseless herding of one hundred-twenty sheep we now would face.

Only now we had Cotton and Uncle Peter to help, and even one of their four dogs that had come limping back to Marietta from wherever it was their sheep had been taken. There was the second wagon, Uncle Peter's, bought back from a Marietta family at half what they paid for it, and all its supplies. Even though we would not have so many sheep to offer at the end of the journey. Father gave the Lesters twenty sheep and the dog that had escaped. They sold Father a saddle horse their neighbors left. He bought the Lester's horse for Moses and me to share. He was apologetic about the sheep dog's paw, but he promised to be back with a better animal on our return.

They were very grateful and pointed out that the dog had already healed mightily during the two days we had been back. And that there was no reason to come this far south on our return.

"Except to see good friends again," Father said.

XXII

After three days' rest with the Lesters, we left their farm on a Monday, the frost on the plowed fields melting in the morning sun. The sheep had fattened considerably in just the few weeks with the Lesters. Against their protests, the Lesters accepted the twenty sheep Father was leaving with them, as study sheep as any. Only the sheep dog we were giving them lacked the robust health of the sheep, and he was fast on the road to recovery.

We would all have been hobbled and lacking considerably had it not been for these settlers and all the Negro settlers across Southern Ohio. We might never have been reunited without their aid.

And now we were together, Uncle Peter and Cotton in their wagon, Father and John Dark Sky in ours, and Moses and I, men we were now, riding herd. Moses rode on ahead as John Dark Sky would have, and I let him delight in being the scout. I knew I would do the same in the next few days. And that neither of us would venture more than a mile or two miles from the flock. That only John Dark Sky or Cotton or Father could drift farther and not fret.

And now, since we were known throughout that part of Ohio, we were dependent on an ever-widening circle of friends.

"Une raison d'etre," Moses called it. And he, on our new horse, came riding back to the flock, pretending not to notice us but to be looking off to his right in the direction we would take the rest of the day. At nothing in particular that I could determine.

We forded the Muskingham River, crunching through the thin ice of its shallow southern fork, and climbed up its far bank to follow it all day to near New Philadelphia. We stayed with the Zoar Community, a harder working group of farmers I could not remember. But they were severe in their dress and stingy in their talk. Nevertheless, they welcomed us and gave us food and hay enough for the animals. And they gave us a barn to house the wagons and horses and mules and ourselves.

They especially welcomed John Dark Sky. It was regrettable to us that for all the trust and human kindness shown by the general run of Ohio settlers, all but a few of them like the Friends, Ohioans seemed to feel they could not trust John Dark Sky. It had not been so when Moses and I were along with him. I recall that those whom we had found most accommodating along the Tuscarawas River trail had been the Negroes. And even some of them seemed hesitant with John Dark Sky.

These Zoar Community people gave no special heed to Moses or Cotton or John Dark Sky. When they spoke to us, it was to all of us, individually or together. They questioned Cotton no less than they questioned Father about the war. They themselves objected to war and were scorned by settlers on surrounding farms, but they were tolerant of Father's service to the Union, as far as we could tell in our short stay with them. And they were no less obliging of John Dark Sky than they were of me or Uncle Peter, and they went out of their way to be certain that all of us would have room enough in the barn.

We remained with the Zoar Community another day. They asked us to speak about our journey and our destination. The Zoarites, having only recently settled here, were divided on whether to remain in Ohio or to go farther west. They sought our reasons for moving on. Some even wondered if others like us would want to settle in their community and if they should welcome non-believers.

Many of their members would gladly have offered us to join them, I believe. Others, it was clear, wanted to move on, like us, to a better life. Theirs was a harsh subsistence, or so they claimed. But the fields looked to be fertile, and ripening with winter wheat, and their equipment and buildings shone with the kind of care only hard-working and well-rewarded caretakers of the land could provide. Still, some were clearly ready to depart for points west, for reasons we could not fathom, if there were reasons.

We did our best to state the purpose of our journey. Father spoke about the desire to aid his friend. Lieutenant Harrison in Wisconsin, about the terrible drought in the East, and about the need to find better farmland. And Father even uttered, for the first time, his discontent over some of the intolerance shown Cotton and Sarah, whom he described as people with a heritage that had been brought to America, a heritage that was not being planted and nurtured and harvested.

What Father didn't say, and what I truly believe was the reason for our journey, was the simple urge to migrate. Maybe it was our heritage; maybe we inherited it from our ancestors. They, like the birds that fly south and return every spring, had followed the deep inner urge to move westward. Was that not what was behind our journey, driving us, as we proceeded?

The Zoar members listened intently to Father's remarks and then left off seeking the reasons for our journey and began to question him and Cotton closely on the Southern attitudes towards Negroes. They themselves had no Negro members among their families but had been considering trading with their Negro neighbors and some were considering inviting Negroes to join in their communal experiment.

We left the kind, hard-working Zoar Community, already in their fields at dawn, and all that day followed the Licking River now open and flowing rapidly with melt, icy only in shadows of overhanging banks of alders and willows.

The third morning, our two wagons left the Licking River at Zanesville and went cross country on the Cumberland Road toward Columbus. The land became hilly, with some steeper climbs but the sun was on the south-facing slopes and the warmth of the midday made us as sleepy as we hadn't been since Western New York, almost sleepy enough to doze off on the wagon seat. And the road, aside from being hilly was rutted by the incessant trail of wagon wheels, sometimes three or four wagons a day heading west, so said a storekeeper in Newark. Several riders on horses passed us and each one bid us a safe journey. There was a spirit of unity in all the movement westward, I can say that with certainty. The approach of their horses and the exchange of friendly greeting woke us up, but we were lulled back into a sleepy gait again after they rode on.

We were men now and could not be caught dozing. And we did not want Uncle Peter and Cotton to notice any flagging of our vigor. John Dark Sky pretended not to notice our tiredness, ever. We were certain of that.

A family we encountered on its way back east on the Cumberland Road thought Columbus could be reached by the next noon. Father thought then to take that afternoon to have a genuine rest and to replenish our supplies and to plot the next phase of our journey.

We pitched our camp for the night on a hilly knoll overlooking a cleared valley divided by the Cumberland Road. Three riders approached our fire in the midst of Father's blessing our evening meal. They paused, still mounted and waited for Father to call the dogs.

Father did call Shep back to the fire and walked to the horsemen. Then he returned, with them afoot, and asked me to hobble their horses. They would be staying for supper.

It soon became apparent that news of our approach to Columbus had preceded us. The three men were a delegation to invite us to participate in Sunday church services at the Congregational church on the town square and to attend the town meeting that afternoon following church. As at the Zoar Community, Father was being asked to speak, the day following, about the war and about our harrowing escape from Morgan's men.

Moses and I were invited to speak also about the aid rendered by the Negroes, our first platform opportunity since debates at school. I looked through my journal and made a few notes, but Moses left our circle around the fire and began braying about his heroics in New Orleans and listing his contributions to every facet of our part in Cotton's escape plan and even adding a few extra deeds and pouring it on about how daring it had all been, and more such theatrics. "Have you always been such a fool?" I asked him, out of earshot of the three men and Father.

"Well, indeed it was more than just the workers at the landing in Portsmouth who helped with Cotton's escape," he said, in the same hortatory tones he was using to address his imagined audience in Columbus.

"If it hadn't been for those landing workers and them alone, there would have been no chance for you to speak, surely," I said. "You might have implored others in Portsmouth, or, if you and I had been less fortunate, we might have explained to authorities in Cincinnati about a steamer that had just crossed to the Kentucky shore with your kidnapped stepfather. That is, we might have explained if we hadn't been kidnapped ourselves."

"Is this doubter?" Moses asked to no one in particular. "Is this the voice of a man? Is this how you see manhood, to have no sureness that you are in control of your fate?" He finally looked at me with a gesture of condescension as he finished.

"All right, Moses, enough. You were brave, yes. You are stronger and braver for having gone through what we went through. Yes. But as far as deserving any credit, wash your mouth out. We did nothing."

"You can say it was nothing, Jesse. It wasn't any nothing. You risked an inconvenience. You were separated from your father and uncle and might have been inconvenienced for a few weeks until they came to get you. Can you know what I risked?"

"No," I said. "No, and neither can you. We can't realize what those settlers risked, what they risk every day. What having been our hosts means. We just went through the motions. They were the conductors. They and their fellows were the ones who risked something."

"You mean you think your father would have been able to sort everything out, save Cotton, save me too, and get us all back together, your Uncle Peter and Cotton and me and you with him?"

Before I could counter him, Father called to us. "Jesse, Moses, come over and talk further to our guests. They want to know you better. Don't be off there by yourselves."

"Yes, sir," Moses said, glaring at me and walking over to the fire.

I shook my head and walked over behind him and sat down next to Father.

"Now explain, Moses you first, and then you Jesse, exactly what happened when you saw Cotton aboard the steamer. Or from the moment you saw him smuggled off. How you felt and how you got back to the settlers' farm" He did not say, "to the Lesters' farm," I noticed.

Moses looked at me and began. "It was all set at Portsmouth landing to get Cotton ashore, you see." As he launched into his version, John Dark Sky stood and walked away from the edge of the fire. "Oh," Moses said, louder, "and John Dark Sky was with us." John Dark Sky walked to the wagon, and then around the wagon, and the horses nickered softly as he approached.

XXIII

Cumberland Road widened through the valley into Columbus. The width of two wagons and then more and more wagons and rigs, enough to pass side by side without one carriage having to edge off the road to the side, the road was that wide, road enough even for the sheep, all 120 sheep together in a flock. A carved sign announced the boundary of the town, as if it couldn't be told from the sudden number of houses, fine houses with curtains and porches and, as we made our way through the traffic and noise, houses on both side of the road, houses with great grassy stretches and gardens leading up to pillared porches.

We drove the sheep on past the capitol building. Men in business attire with top hats and greatcoats went in and out even on this, a Saturday. It was a far cry from the dusty trails and rolling farmlands we had grown used to.

Father stopped our procession at a board walkway that curved around a corner into a hotel. "Men, let's take some rooms and get baths. It has been a long time," Father said.

A hotel! Baths inside the rooms! Running water!

Moses let out a squeak of delight and hopped down off the horse. He sailed up the wooden stairs and into the lobby before I could turn the mules across the road to the livery where a buckboard driver was unhitching his horse.

When John Dark Sky and I had paddocked the horses and turned the mules into the corral behind the livery, I looked across the road, preparing in my mind's eye a steaming bath and luxurious bed and china plates for our dinner. I just hoped Moses hadn't beat me to the bath.

I unfolded my new shirt, only worn once since Christmas, a stiff pair of dress pants, now too short, but upon last wearing, not too snug around the waist, and my coat. I came around the back of the wagon to ask John Dark Sky if he could tie down the wagon flaps and I saw him extend a hand to Cotton. Cotton first handed up a bedroll to John Dark Sky, then mounted the seat next to him.

It puzzled me. Cotton had taken out his bedding, but he would be sleeping between pressed sheets with blankets, if not under a featherbed. It occurred to me that neither Cotton nor John Dark Sky brought out their fine clothes for the hotel.

I tucked my shirt, my pants, and my coat under one arm and crossed the road, stepped up the board stairs and entered the darkened lobby of the hotel. Overstuffed chairs were arranged around a fire spitting sparks in a floor-to-ceiling fireplace. In the corner, a bar was occupied by an overweight gentleman in a frockcoat and watch chain and a taller gentleman in a cap, smoking a cigar.

Moses came down the stairs two at a time and hopped over next to me and took my clothes. "What are you doing?" I asked.

"Taking your things, sir," he said, looking around him and over his shoulder at the same time.

Something was amiss. When had Moses ever taken anything for me? I reached to take back what he had arranged over one arm, but he was already skipping back to the staircase. "You are in room number 27," he called.

I took two steps toward the second floor stairs when I cried out, "No!" and stopped abruptly. "No, Moses, come back."

I looked up through the banisters, but Moses had already disappeared. I turned back, intending to stride back through the lobby and out of the smoke-filled hotel. The men at the bar stared with seeming disinterest at me. I stopped. Then I turned and went back up the stairs, more slowly, thinking what I could do to stop this from happening.

Father and Uncle Peter were standing outside a room in the hall. Moses was looking out from the doorway of a room next to theirs. I reached father's side and before I could say a word, he said, "We are here to rest, Jesse. I know you realize we should not, under the circumstances, but to give us the strength we need, we must accept this."

What could I do? I could leave. I could go to Cotton and John Dark Sky and sleep in the cold wagon or in the livery with the horses. We had done no less the entire trip and had done happily. Or I could accept this insult and let Moses pretend to be my valet or whatever he called himself so he could stay in the room.

I shrugged and passed by Father and Uncle Peter and walked into the room. Moses had stripped off his clothing already and laid it in folds in the center of the room on a braided rug. The door was ajar between our room and Uncle Peter and Father's room. Doors passed into a common bath, and Moses was in that closet, filling a copper tub with water from a kettle. He returned the kettle, filled, to andirons in the fireplace. I sat down on the bed. It was hopeless. Truly this was unjust.

Father came into the room. "Jesse, understand I feel as you do that is not right. Believe me when I say that Cotton and John Dark Sky wish us to have these rooms. They will be much easier not having to be excluded except as they choose."

"I can't say yes, no, I don't know the best thing," I said. I lay back on the bed and looked up at the ceiling. A painted cherub stared down at me. Pink and naked with wings and curly locks of hair. The painted scene faded into the darkness of the moldings at the corners of the ceiling.

"You remember I mentioned there would be hard parts of the journey," Father was saying. "Having Uncle Peter imprisoned and Cotton's freedom imperiled was hard. This is harder yet. We can do nothing about it as guests here. We resist in our minds and let our soreness be soothed by the comforts here."

I heard a kettle roiling in the next room and knew that Moses was boiling enough water to add to the bathwater. Father went to the bath to help Moses pour. I heard Moses splashing in the water and saw steam come from the bath. Then I heard Father refill the kettle and replace in on the andirons. My eyes closed and I fell asleep listening to Moses splash in the tub.

I awoke sometime in the middle of the night. I had been covered over with a comforter and someone, Father perhaps, had removed my boots and wrapped the comforter around my stocking feet. Moses was asleep beside me, smelling of scented soap. I rose up to go to the wagon. I could not stay here. I would walk out in the night stockingfooted if my boots were not outside the door. I would take my place beside the men whose respect I felt had been violated. I would not live the shame brought to them and to us.

It was dawn when I awoke again, still wrapped in the comforter. So I had fallen asleep again. And it was morning. And I had slept while Cotton and John Dark Sky had been curled up in a cold wagon. I knew I was not evil but could do nothing about it. Not now, perhaps not ever.

We dressed and went to the hotel dining hall for breakfast. Moses for some reason was seated with us and I wondered whether we might not add John Dark Sky and Cotton. Father saw my bewilderment and said, "We will take a full tray of foods to Cotton and John Dark Sky. They will be fed as we are fed."

I ate, as I had slept, with great need. I overate. I stuffed myself. Moses was filling a plate again with sausages and grits and filling his cup with coffee from a glass coffee urn.

Father requested, and was brought, a tray of biscuits, a gravy boat, roasted eggs broken into a cream sauce, a bowl with grits, and a pitcher of coffee. Metal covers kept the food warm. Linen napkins and china cups and plates, a pair of silver knives and forks completed the tray. Father excused himself, took this tray, and walked through the dining room and out through the door into the lobby.

Moments later, he returned to finish his coffee and fold his napkin. A Negro waiter cleared our plates and the serving dishes. He winked at Moses and gave him a nudge as Moses and I pushed our chairs back into place.

"That man was enjoying his work," Moses said. "He was delighted to take your Father's coin. So don't look at me in the disapproving tone."

"Pray we can live through this and then forget it happened," I said.

"Why? Why should we forget a thing? Write it down. Write how you feel, Jesse. If you feel downtrodden, if you feel violated. Write it down. Then you might have one, miniscule inkling of what the experience of being a Negro is. Write down what I did. And write down what you hear this afternoon at that church meeting. You will hear all the best promises of making it right by us, and not one will come true. You will hear vainglory boasting of emancipating us from our savage pasts. Write down what is said from the pulpit if that is where we speak. Write is all down. And maybe one day what you wrote will be a record of shame, and that shame might just make a difference in the way a Negro is treated."

We had grown up and we had been growing up so differently for all that we were growing up together. Moses was growing proud, so proud he could mock himself and mock conventions and not be affected in the least. I was growing dismayed. For all the weeping and fighting and swearing, there was not a thing I could do to heal what had become a sickness this nation had. I could drive the sheep westward, on and on, and keep them from straying too far, and keep them on the course. Moses could be with me on the journey. But we were not on the same journey. It was best to realize that now, and together, for the time being, to keep the sheep on the road westward.

XXIV

CHURCH MEETINGS SMELL the same, parish halls smoke from downdrafts, and crowded with woolens drying from snow or rain. Worst of all, baked dishes for the socials, where every bit of food is the same cabbage-smelling fare. I appreciated the warmth in my stomach, but it soon became too warm in the parish hall where over eighty souls were chewing their meals and talking about new settlements and the lack of game and other problems that came with having a thoroughfare running into and out of a town.

Moses spoke the longest, about our adventure on the Ohio River, and we each retold it several times after the official speeches. The people of Columbus had good intentions, and, except for the hosteller, their every instinct seemed honorable. But for all their goodness and loving kindness, and for all the courtesy they extended to each of us during that church meeting, they still had in their midst, a hotel that was not prepared to extend the same courtesies to all. It was not something that could be explained. It had to be felt, and they showed no feeling one way or the other. These were good people. It made me wonder if my feelings were selfish, if I was the one who was misguided.

It was a warm reception for us and the various offers to house us for the night were genuine. Father declined each offer politely explaining how early we must be setting off the next day. February was ending and spring was being ushered in on a warming south wind.

We gathered with a few townspeople for their suggestions for travel westward. Father was in favor of continuing along the Cumberland Road to Dayton. From Dayton, a road north would be easy enough to follow.

But the plan that we eventually settled on was spoken first by a Negro butler, one of the household servants of a prominent Columbus banker. The butler and Cotton conversed outside the church as they awaited our dismissal.

"Mr. Reeves suggests we travel by the river course," Cotton reported. And then Mr. Reeves, the butler, drew the course for us on stationery kept in a desk that he called a secretary in the banker's carriage.

After a second night of discomforted rest in the uncivil hotel, I felt a sense of relief as we left Columbus. The days when we had traveled the Cumberland Road, we had had a well-traveled surface and our wagons fairly sailed along like the prairie schooners. But our sheep had presented one problem after another from Zanesville to Columbus. They tended out in a widespread arc away from the wagon to search for grasses, and they caused no end of inconvenience when any other wagon or carriage came along, especially as we neared Columbus. Tired as we were, we had to clear both lanes of the roadway, then gather our sheep back from the fields where they had scattered.

And the stretch of the Cumberland Road into Columbus had afforded no satisfactory place to overnight the sheep. Even in a town the size of Columbus there was difficulty. The town livery offered scarcely enough extra space in its corral for our mules, the town green was unacceptable with the next day's church service and meeting, and the town itself was spread out so far along the road that a good mile from the hotel was the first suitable enclosed pasture for the sheep.

Thus, our new Scioto River course, bumpy though it was already, was a far sight easier than the likes of the Cumberland Road for driving sheep. The flock could wander the banks of the Scioto River, its icy edges beginning to thaw in Columbus, and we would not concern ourselves with any strays crossing the open river. Nor would the sheep stray far afield to the west. No sooner did we leave Columbus than we came upon dense woods growing to the trail's edge, and where the occasional settler had cleared his property, the sheep were herded along the trail by our dogs. Between clearings the sheep wandered through woods, and we wove our way as best we could with the few other wagons on the narrow river road.

For some unknown reason, perhaps it was a discomfort about our safety, Moses and I both were feeling a good share sharper as we drove the sheep up along the Scioto River. It was foolish to think there was danger from Indian attack along this lonely, wooded trail. The few remaining Indians were peaceful farmers. The first day's travels took us past settlers' cabins now and again, and the settlers seemed friendly. Uncle Peter and Cotton survived the worst of times along the Musingham River, and Cotton, even worse on the steamboat. This untrafficked Scioto River, represented no threat save what lurked in our imaginations.

We kept sharp for any eventuality, nonetheless. None came. None to speak of. The second and third days along the Scioto River were eventless. I took no notes in my journal. The days grew longer and once again, Moses and I began to relax and doze in the duties, alternating as passengers and drives on uncle Peter's wagon or Father's wagon as we rolled along the settlers' buckboard ruts, the main markings of the route north from Columbus.

Where the Scioto River turns west, we brought the wagons closer together and pitched camp on a bend in the road for our third night north of Columbus. For the last two of these days, we had seen no other travelers and only scarcely a settler in his field. Wagon ruts, the signs of other traffic, all but disappeared.

As Moses and I hobbled the horses for the night, a rig lurched towards us from the west. A series of oaths at top volume were voiced before I could make out the driver of the wagon in the growing darkness. The worst looking wagon imaginable clattered to a halt at our campsite. A bearded driver wearing the least tidy costume I had ever seen reined in a barrel-shaped gray pony.

We hailed the driver as he descended by stepping gingerly on a loose spoke, lifting his foot to fend off our barking dogs, hollering back at the dogs in a steady stream of lewd invective. His tirade continued even after Father, none too quickly it seemed, called off the dogs.

"Those consarned, devil-toothed hounds better not chew on me or they'll die of distemper," he roared.

"Good evening," Father offered. "Have a mug of coffee?"

"Don't mind if I do," said the driver, scratching his bald head. "Been some kinda day. First, the bridge is out; then my best customer dies; and last, the constabulary invites me out of the very premises where I last performed to a packed house."

"Are you an actor then?" Uncle Peter asked.

"Why, yes I be, and a healer too. Let's see that there hand. Could use a little faith to fix that up? Oh, I see, a little more'n faith, I reckon then. That there was a bad 'un. War was it?" He accepted father's coffee.

Uncle Peter said nothing, but nodded slightly.

"Welps," the man continued, "what difference does it make if I give it away? Have some of my medicine. Good for ghost pain in missing limbs or in them that's still attached." He howled with laughter and went to his rig. He set Father's mug, still steaming, on the seat and reached behind the seat to withdraw a bottle.

"Here." He returned to the fire with the coffee and the bottle. He took a sip of coffee and dribbled some out on his beard as he said, "A little goes a long way," handing the bottle to Uncle Peter.

Uncle Peter politely took the bottle, holding its bluish contests to the firelight.

"You mentioned a bridge out?" Father asked the man.

"I should guess so. Burned out by Red devils, 'scues me for sayin' so." He looked at John Dark Sky. "Not your people, certain, my friend," he said to John Dark Sky. "Just some Indians hot about the settlers taking more of their land. The usual gripe. I wouldn't give a wooden nickel for all the settlers in Ohio. Indians are better by a long sight than people clearing all the good woods and ruinnin' the waterways with their slops.

"Bridge? I should say," he went on, "and two, three cabins and a stable. Stole horses too, I heared said. The devils."

"On the Scioto River this all was?" Father asked, ignoring the man's oaths, which surprised me more than Father's apparent hospitality.

"The Scioto no. The Auglaize, up to Lima, or near, where the two Auglaizes come together. That the way you'll be headin'?"

"It might be," Father said, hedging. But of course it was the very way the butler had drawn for us.

"Well, you can get to a mile or so from the crossing, but from there into Lima there's no way but to go 'round. Your might's well head north here and then west if'n you're bound for Lima. Say, can you spare a little of that coffee?"

Father refilled the man's mug and bid him sit for supper with us. Father's hospitality knew no bounds. The man greedily sat over a plate and devoured a portion of Cotton's stew. We would have to fish for breakfast. Several dozen fish would be needed if this man was to be our guest for breakfast too.

But to my amazement, the actor rose, belched, and thanked us for the meal. "I don't mean nothin' 'bout Indians and coloreds," he said. "You can't find better people, 'cept some of the colored settlers, of course. If they cook as good food as you," he said to Cotton, "they can settle all of Ohio 'n Indiana they want. Much obliged to you, and," he added, turning to Uncle Peter, "don't forget to say the little ditty on the bottle when you take a sup, and if you can't say it then you better lay off it for a spell," and he cackled.

"Good evening and thank you. Boys." He rose and bowed and returned to his buckboard.

John Dark Sky had fed the man's gray pony and had removed burrs from its tail during the man's description of the bridge at Lima.

"Good luck," said Father, and we waved goodbye as the man lurched off at a rattling pace and disappeared in the gloom down the Scioto River trail.

After we cleaned and returned the supper pans to the wagon, Father said, "You stand the first watch, Peter."

XXV

A NEW MOON WAS setting when Moses shook me for my turn at watch. I got up and washed my face in the cold, open water along the margin of the Scioto River. Shadows from the branches faded from its surface and the sky became thicker with stars. I kicked a log onto the fire and sparks showered upwards to the stars. Somewhere raccoons screeched and then screeched more.

I was thinking of our Hudson River and the ships that plied is currents, and here we were by this trickle of a river. Whatever the size of the Auglaize River, since it had a bridge burned out or not, it couldn't compare to the Hudson. Moses was determined to show me the Mississippi River up in Wisconsin, not a day's ride from Boscobel. "Now that," he would often say, "is a river. Even the Hudson is but another of these little Ohio rivers compared to the Mississippi," he claimed. "And that goes for the Ohio River as well."

To me, the Ohio was almost as far across as the Hudson, and if there was a river that made it seem small, I would like to see that river.

I watched the stars slide down the sky and poked up the fire more. We might get to the Mississippi River someday, but just to get to Wisconsin was journey enough to me. We still had three states to go, and we weren't even out of Ohio. The thought of going any farther than we had already gone was enough to make me wish I was home on our hillside overlooking the river in the little chicken coop of a cabin I loved, not here in a freezing wildness on an endless trek westward.

Father arose and stepped out of the wagon. He wrapped his blanket tighter and came over to the fire. Cotton too was rising.

"Good morning, Father," I said. "Everything is calm."

"Jesse, I wonder if you know how much I admired you, back in Columbus." Father was about to praise me for something I felt utterly lacking in, something I was ashamed of. "You and Moses are good friends, the closest two young men I have yet observed. Closer than Peter and I were. You admire each other, and I am proud to see you growing up together and gaining manhood."

I lifted the pot onto the grate to boil water and added a branch to the fire. "We have a few disagreements," I said, "but we make up for them."

Father waited as the water heated. "I realize you were in a compromising position." He shifted the pot more onto the center of the grate. "Moses could see how much it hurt you to resign yourself to the hotel practices. By showing him how you felt, you did more than any going out to sleep in our wagon could have done. Do you see that?"

"I see it. It is not fair, though."

"It may never be fair even though President Lincoln has tried, and the war has tried to make better opportunities for all people. People like those in the church in Columbus are fair, and they are the ones who will see to the changes in their own midst."

"If they don't do as I did, they can change things," I replied.

"Let us hope you will not have to do again something that goes so against your nature. Let us pray more of us resist." He looked up as Cotton knelt at the river's edge, collecting water for our meal.

The water came to a boil and Father added coffee to the pot and set it again on the grate. John Dark Sky came into the firelight. I had not heard him stirring, but he looked to have been up a considerable time. Father gave him and Cotton each a mug of coffee, and John Dark Sky handed Father a pouch full of duck eggs.

'"I am surprised they nested so soon," Father said. "This is an earlier spring here, what do you think?"

He waited a full minute before replying. "Spring seems cooler. More snow will help the planting. It is good for all animals in the cold."

John Dark Sky was right, of course. If animals survive the winter and crops survive the cold nights, they will be hardier and better able to withstand droughts and harsh weather. I wondered if we were becoming hardier in our wandering. Would we be able to survive harsh conditions?

Then perhaps here was reason for such obstacles. Perhaps this was a reason for the journey. But what harsh circumstances would we yet face. And would they weaken us or further strengthen us?

Uncle Peter stepped down from his wagon, and Moses stretched and stood on the seat of our wagon. Cotton came back to the fire to fry pork to scramble the five eggs. "Your father is right. Moses knows how much you care for each other," Cotton said.

"I know," I said. "Columbus was a poor way for me to have shown him though."

We packed the wagons and were dousing the fire when three riders approached from the west. They looked at the ground where the wheels of our visitor's rig stopped the night before.

"Good day, gentlemen. Did you have the pleasure of meeting Mr. Flanagan yesterday?"

"If he be the bearded actor who passed here, yes," said Father.

The men looked at one another. "He is an actor, in truth," said the middle rider. "He acted up enough to ruffle some feathers in Lima. They say he is responsible for several women's discomfort and perhaps for some of their missing valuables. We are from the Lima town council, merely trying to persuade him to return the valuables. If he has them."

One of the men rode past and examined the trail where it turned south. "Did he leave this morning or last night?" He called to Father from where he was examining the trail.

It was not our pleasure to enjoy his company overnight," Father said. "He'll be a day's travel on down the road, I imagine."

"Much obliged," the third rider said, tipping his hat. "We'll be on our way. Safe journey." The three walked their horses along the trail going south for a ways, then trotted their mounts out of sight.

I felt sorry for Mr. Flanagan. He was, after all, acting out his role as what Father calls a rounder. He should not have taken the valuable items, though. Unless the women offered them to him as Father had offered him supper. His was a certain contagious charm that made everything seem livelier, fresher. I hoped he might return the valuables and be let off.

We set off following the Scioto River for ten miles as it gently flowed south. Then John Dark Sky rode back from being gone all morning and reported a cleared trail across country to a place where a river, he thought it was the Auglaize, could be forded. We were one mile south of Lima, where we thought to stay the night, but Father and Uncle Peter decided to head west. Across the Auglaize River, the way John Dark Sky suggested.

It was a winding, westward trek, keeping the stray sheep from venturing too far into the woods, backtracking on our trail at times to find a way around impassable thickets, and pushing the wagons over logs. The trail took us up a low hill to a rocky descent into a valley. We wound around the hill, avoiding boulders, and came along the base of a cliff.

Darkness was approaching and I wondered when we would be stopping when John Dark Sky pointed to a place where boulders had fallen away from the cliff, and where birds were flying in and out. Bats. A cave, not far above our heads, and an easy climb.

"Can we explore, Father?" I begged, and Moses was already off his horse and ready to pounce on the boulders.

"Go on," Father said to Moses, who had already mounted the first boulder on his way to the cave. "Just watch for bears." And Moses stopped atop a boulder, near at the mouth of the cave, staring down at me.

I joined a much more cautious Moses and tentatively, together, we entered the cave, stooping to avoid overhanging vines. The others had stopped and were unloading the supplies for the evening meal. So we should have a little time to make our survey of the cave.

It was smaller than I hoped, and dark, too dark to make much out. But we heard the dripping of water somewhere toward the back of the cave. "Let's get a torch and map this proper," I said.

"I'll just hop down and make one and you can stay here" Moses said.

"It's no trouble," I said. "I'll go with you and borrow the flint and tinder so we can make a fire," I said.

"A good idea," Moses agreed. And we exited the cave, breathing a little better.

We helped gather the supper things and ate quickly. Father shooed us off afterward, and, with the gray of evening coming on, we returned to the cave, torch ready and the makings of kindling for a fire.

Once back inside the cave, we struck the torch and saw a pool of water a few inches deep and a crevice, too narrow for us, into which a bat flew. We looked around at the walls of the cave and decided we had seen enough.

"Try drinking the water, Moses," I suggested. He took my challenge and scooped some up in his hand. He turned and spit out as soon as he tasted it.

"Sulfur!" he exclaimed. "It tastes like rotten eggs."

My courage was not up to his. But I bent over and made as if to taste it. "Ummm!" I said, in mock approval. "Delicious, is it not?"

The water did have an unpleasant smell, and I was glad I had only smelled it. Later that night, as we lay in the wagon after our excursion to the cave, Moses said, "I must confess, I was too put off to taste any of the cave water. I only pretended to spit it out."

"I didn't taste it either," I said. "It smelled bad."

"I thought you hadn't," Moses said. "But don't fool me, agreed?"

"I agree. You fooled me though. Let's make a pact not to, from now on."

"A pact," Moses said. But I was sure we would go back on our word.

XXVI

Through the valley and across a clear plain, we drove the dutiful sheep, our two wagons pulled by tireless mules. I wondered what we looked like – six dogs and three horses, and four men, no six men counting Moses and me. Six men and half a nation to cross. Moses rode ahead with John Dark Sky, and Father and Uncle Peter each at the wagon reins, leaving me and Cotton to drive the sheep. It was no chore as the land stretched out before us. Grassy shoots were appearing along the banks of streams and clumps of sorrel grass slowed the sheep as they mowed their way across the valleys.

Moses rode back to announce, "There is a river up yonder," pointing to the line of trees north one half mile.

Father had commented on it as a possibility when we first saw the trees, but he kept to the valley. To allow the sheep their grass, I imagined.

But we turned towards the trees now, and shortly we came to a wide, shallow river flowing in a straight line from the northwest. We drank from it and I skinned down and swam a few strokes in its frigid current. When I rubbed down with a blanket and jumped back into my clothes, Father handed me a cup of broth. Cotton had collected shoots of onion grass and dandelion greens and boiled it with fish he caught. The broth was savory and warmed me quickly.

We dallied at the river, called the St. Mary's River we learned when we arrived at Fort Wayne in Indiana the next week, after our four-day journey along its banks.

The St. Mary's River was a broad floodplain, but this spring the melt was less than usual we learned, and the river was well within its banks, even low enough in the few turns it took for the sandy banks to extend out like beaches. These soft, sandy shores, stretching well out into the river as it began to turn north gave us the pleasant remembrance of the Esopus Island shore. Moses joined me in my next day's dip into its numbing eddies, and, once we were in, challenged me to race to the far bank. We both set out in a dozen flailing overhand strokes before we decided to turn back and even more quickly to return to the shore, gasping and aching with cold.

Father and Cotton laughed at our antics, but even they ventured in to their waists and joined us on our next swim. At about the time March was ending, we came into April and passed into Indiana. There was no distinct sign in the landscape, no benchmark along the river, no change in the appearance of the river or of the settlers' cabins. "I shall be glad to get shut of Ohio once and for all," I said to Moses as we lay in the sun to warm up after another of our swims, the fourth day along the St. Mary's River.

"We may be in Indiana already," he said. Cotton thinks so, and John Dark Sky said the homesteader he spoke to back at the fork in the river thought it was Indiana, although he wasn't sure where the line was drawn."

"What do you think of that?" I said. "A man clearing land he will claim and building a cabin on a river he might not know the name of, not even sure what state he is in."

"On the Mississippi River it was that way in spring floods. We could be in Louisiana or Mississippi either, the water confused the land so."

"If we are in Indiana, I'll say a prayer of thanks for safe passage out of Ohio," I said.

"We mightn't be free of Ohio," Moses said. "We have to go back again one day."

"Maybe there's a better way," I offered. "Maybe a northern route, through Canada. Or maybe I'll just keep going around the world and get back easier that way than going back through Ohio."

"We know what to expect now," Moses said, "and where the good people can be found. Besides, we have to go back to the Lesters and pay our respects."

"You are right. It wouldn't do to go back and not return to visit them. I'll allow you that."

"When you write down about Ohio in your journal," Moses said, "be sure to mark the treats as well as the tricks along the way. We may need to study it to keep to the way that treated us better."

I do not know at what point, what tree or what turn in the river, I began to want to be home. Something about the spring and the banks along the St. Mary's river beginning to green made me wonder about how big Ruth would be. Would she be big enough to sit in front of us in the saddle? I wished we could be back to make the first dive of the spring into Black Creek at the waterfall and raft over to Esopus Island on the Hudson River.

"Moses," I asked, "do you ever miss school?"

"I do. I was just thinking about the school meetings. I miss everybody and being quiet and thinking hard all together."

"Only now it would be vacation time. It is Easter tomorrow, Father said. I don't miss getting my knuckles rapped for pulling Prudence Hurd's braids," I said.

Moses laughed. "She didn't tell when I pulled them," he said. "It must be that she wanted all the others to know that you were interested in her."

"She is pretty," I said. "But her braids knocked my quill off the desk. I guess she might have done it on purpose."

"I wish we could be back on the river," Moses said.

"I miss the rafting. It was fine bumping among the ice floes and tying up at Esopus Island in March."

"I think about Easter and the egg hunt in Kingston on the green last year," Moses said. "I found the purple egg."

We rode in silence then. When it was our turn to take the wagons, I thought about the duck eggs John Dark Sky found. Cotton cooked all but four. Could we find a dye to make Easter eggs, I wondered. And how might we make Easter baskets?

Moses' mind must have been turning over the same ideas, for when we stopped for the night, both of us went to the larder box in Cotton's wagon to see about the eggs.

The sun was setting later and later and after our evening meal, we still had light enough to search for an egg dye. Moses came up with a yew berry that gave a pink glow when it was crushed and spread on a stone. I found holly berries, but they would not yield a color when we tried boiling them. Cotton had the best solution: saffron he gathered from the crocuses that were in bloom. It made a dark yellow stain on the eggshells.

And so we made golden eggs for our Easter, one each for Cotton, Uncle Peter, John Dark Sky and Father. Father made small rush baskets for Moses and me and placed in the baskets licorice and peppermint drops he had carried all the way from Marietta. Rabbits galore ran about in the woods, and so we had our Easter bunnies and all their families dancing all the Easter day through.

We climbed trees to look around the countryside. A new growth of maples and pines had grown up after logging had cleared the woods a few years before, when the railroad was completed. A few grand old trees remained, tall pines and oaks, and the new growth was thicker in the older cleared areas. Father said they would need to be thinned to grow trees as tall as the great oaks we camped among.

In a small, quiet ceremony before our Easter meal, Father offered a prayer for our safety and thanks for the reuniting of this much of our family. He said words for the wellbeing of Sarah and Ruth, and he blessed Moses and me. It was a long prayer and I was hungry enough to wish he had skipped some of it. The blessing of Moses and me was pleasant to hear, though, and I was glad to know Father still gave such blessings. I accepted it coming through prayer as though it had come directly from Father. It was simply not his way to thank anyone directly to his face. I know he was pleased that Moses and I were along. Many times we were helpful, not only at the crucial time of Cotton's escape. All the times we rode our turns in the nighttime drives in New York, the times we took our watch in Ohio, and certainly the times we brought in fish, especially the muskellunge, he must have been happy. So it was good to hear a blessing.

I didn't know if sons could bless their fathers, but I did anyway. I blessed Father, quietly, not out loud. He had brought us on the long adventure and trusted us to serve for him when he had departed to look for Uncle Peter, and now more and more, he was giving us credit for being grown, men in our own right. I believe he would accept a blessing from a son. I hoped he would. He was, of all fathers, most deserving.

I blessed John Dark Sky too. For the assurance he brought us all.

The next morning, before the sun even topped the tallest oak in our grove, we were up and packing our things and rounding the sheep into a tight drive. The day was warm, with a soft breeze wrinkling the water. The riverbank ran straight through the woods, pointing our way and providing us with a gentle laughter as it ran over rocks.

We could go on like this many days, so I was almost saddened to see the rooftops of houses circling the garrison at Fort Wayne. There would be beds and fresh supplies, new friends for Moses and me to meet, stories of the war from troops shipping in and out. But for all the distractions I would miss the peaceful days of driving the sheep along this graceful river. I would count these as some of the moments most pleasant to remember on our long passage, and I would lie awake nights when I was too tired to sleep and think back on these days of our riding along the St. Mary's River as a time when all the troubles of our travels were behind us. I was glad for these days.

Wagons of all descriptions and scores of horses and mules, and a huge pen of cattle, and another with sheep and goats surrounded the gates of Fort Wayne. Even though there were fewer than one hundred soldiers, it looked as if the entire migration west had come for supplies and letters from dear ones back east or south or from whichever direction they had come.

We were just gathering our supper cooking pans and laying a fire when Father came back with his arms laden. A twenty pound sack of flour, another of corn meal, two rows of sausages, a jar of molasses, and a headless rooster still dripping blood.

"Roast chicken for supper," Cotton said, rubbing his hands together.

Father set the supplies in the back of the wagon and Moses went about plucking the rooster. Father brought more than food, though. "Richmond is surrounded," he reported. Further west, the Confederate Army was in retreat, with General Grant pursuing. "It may be a prolonged end, but it is the end, surely," Father said. "Many a Northern soldier will be passing through here next year on the way home."

We said prayers for the safe return of all soldiers, Northern, and, as father always added, Southern. For although he was deeply committed to ending slavery and reuniting the nation, he was a deeply concerned about each man and family in the nation. "We are all brothers," he would say, "friends and enemies."

Could we pray for John Hunt Morgan's varmints, then? I decided we could not pray for their deeds to be forgiven, but we could pray that they would aright themselves in the Creator's eyes and in the eyes of their fellow man. And if that meant they would go safely back to their Southern lives in peace, then I could pray for them too. But it was not in my nature to want to pray for them, and I am not certain I actually did. But I prayed often a prayer of thanks for our safe passage.

I fell asleep that night feeling completely safe for the first time since Christmas Eve at the Presque Inn. The fire glowed and the baked chicken was still rich on the air around our wagons. Father's voice was quietly rising and falling as he and John Dark Sky talked to a sergeant about the best route to take west. My stomach was full and my thoughts were peaceful. The night was warm enough so I was only using one blanket, and the sheep were safely penned outside the fort. Shep seemed to feel the peace of the evening as well, for he lay beside the wagon, his head on both paws, his eyes barely able to stay open. He had been at work all these months without rest and looked thinner in spite of his winter coat. We all required this rest, and when I awoke in the middle of the night, I heard snores from John Dark Sky's wagon, the only time I remembered a sound of sleep from his quarter. Maybe it was Cotton though.

I was the first one up in the morning, and I prodded the fire and blew it into a flame, adding some cedar twigs John Dark Sky had gathered. John Dark Sky stood between the wagons and stretched. He would not need to search ahead for a trail for us today. Father would follow the army's best route.

North, at least for half the day, before turning west – that had been the sergeant's recommendation. We followed a stream called the St. Joseph River northward until the sun was directly over us, and then we turned the sheep across country, through hills and down through a broad valley past lakes with the first insects of the spring dancing above their waters. The sheep were taking longer going, grazing as we went, but the pace bothered neither Father nor Uncle Peter. We were enjoying the springtime.

XXVII

"ONE LONG CHAIN of lakes and streams" was what I wrote about Indiana in my journal. We passed few settlements and encountered almost no travelers. There were days when we saw no one. We had plentiful fish for ourselves from the lakes, and marsh grasses were provender for our sheep. The mules and horses began looking less gaunt. Shep and the other dogs were shedding and looked shabby, but our more relaxed pace seemed to put new strength and life into them.

Our path diverted around the small lakes and we crossed and recrossed many streams that spun a large web out around us. Although the wagon became stuck more than once, the mules, with Boca and John Dark Sky's horse helping, towed it back onto firm ground. Rain fell almost every Sunday it seemed. There were no churches to worship, and so Father conducted prayer and read scriptures in the wagon by lamplight those wet Sundays.

Moses became restless, and his jumpiness put all of us at sixes and sevens. I wanted to sleep or write or read, but Moses was for exploring.

"What is there to see that we haven't already seen?" I finally asked on a dark Sunday, after Father's readings had ended.

"How can I know unless I see for myself?" he answered. And off he rode to the north, to find only more lake country, more marshes. When he came back from one evening ride, he brought back a painted turtle. At first the dogs pestered the turtle, but they gave up after little success at perturbing it. Eventually it lumbered away in the direction we were taking, northwest.

"We are making about as much progress as my turtle," Moses observed later that night as we were tucking the blankets around us.

"Better to have a direction to follow like the turtle," I said. "Those rabbits that skip back and forth get nowhere. We're almost to Wisconsin."

"I wonder when," Moses said.

"Be patient, Moses," I said. "Maybe we'll be there by Christmas."

"Don't make light of it," Moses scolded. "I don't feature another hot summer of traveling by night and suffering through endless days of no sleep."

"We're going to make it, and before Independence Day," I promised.

"Not before the war is over, I'd say." Moses blew out the lamp.

One of the days we bogged down several times, Father's wagon became mired again towards evening, in a field that had sinkholes. Father looked at the axle, resting on a crumbling limestone ledge and at the wheel that had become wedged in the sudden cave-in.

"I think the axle may be broken, this time," he said, looking down the shaft to the hub of the wheel. The wagon chassis had remained above the surface putting great tension on the axle.

"So even when we tow it out, we might have to have a new axle," Uncle Peter said, finishing the thought that Father had started.

"We'll rest here for the night and take another look at dawn," Father said. "This is a piece of bad luck, but we can always go on with one wagon, if need be. Let us see about bracing the frame for the night."

John Dark Sky and Cotton fashioned a lever from the trunk of a cedar Father cut down, which they had forced the trunk under the axle at the elevated end of the wagon. Then they drove Uncle Peter's wagon so the end was under our raised right front edge to support the weight of our wagon.

We began to offload our wagon because we would need it lighter to tow it out of the sinkhole. Our clothing and whiskey and what was left of the whale oil, John Dark Sky's deerskins hides, lamps, Father's rifle, blankets, and the bags of flour an corn meal were set outside and covered with the canvas fly.

Cotton prepared more of the rabbit stew that had become our staple. The game was abundant, and the fish fairly leapt out of the streams and onto our line in these Indiana streams. We slept outside the wagon soundly on cedar boughs John Dark Sky cut from the cedar levered under our wagon. I inhaled the sweet odor of the greens all night. And we wrapped ourselves tightly in blankets against the night dew.

In the morning, the sky was overcast, and after a breakfast that was a reprise of Cotton's good stew, ("even better the second day," I said) we set about releasing our wagon from the ground's hold. Father and John Dark Sky lashed ropes from the rear axle of our wagon to their saddle horns and the mules were led behind the wagon and hitched there to a makeshift singletree Cotton fashioned from a stout pine branch. We would attempt to pull the wagon backwards, back up and onto the solid part of the ledge we were on.

With Cotton and Uncle Peter heaving on the cedar limb levered even more tightly under our front axle, and with the mules and horses tugging from behind, the wagon lurched slowly up and almost clear of the hole. Then the axle snapped. The front of the wagon slipped off Uncle Peter's wagon and went down on the limb Uncle Peter and Cotton held on their shoulders and the front wheel broke entirely free.

The wagon remained upright, but leaned badly onto its broken front corner. Uncle Peter and Cotton had not been hurt, nor had the wagon suffered any further damage, but as it was now, it was useless to us.

Father looked tiredly at the wreckage and began to unload the rest of the wagon, the hay, a box of shells, cooking pots, the rest of the apples in their barrel. Cotton rearranged his things and we packed as much of our supplies as would fit into the corners and on top of his and Uncle Peter's belongings. And we detached the broken front axle to match it, we hoped, to another like enough to it to replace ours.

What we could not take, the cooking things we would not need, the winter clothing, John Dark Sky's deerskins, the whale oil we were going to give the Harrisons, the apple barrel, the hay, we put back into our wagon. If we could find another axle along the way and make use of it to replace ours, it might be possible to retrieve our wagon. Father did not seem to despair. There was not much else to do except what we were doing.

"It is fortunate we are traveling together, Peter," Father said, when all the goods were transferred. "This way we will lose, at the worse, what we have left. And the wagon. But we may find a smith to repair this axle."

I wondered how far Father would be willing to travel before he would not consider returning to our wagon. Two days? Two weeks? And even if another axle or a sleeve for this one could be found, would it work?

We set off at noon, leaving the wagon that had been our home these many months behind, leaning badly to the south. John Dark Sky would stay one week at most, to guard the wagon in the event it could be repaired. At that week's end, if there were no word, he would ride to meet us somewhere along the Lake Michigan shore. They looked forlorn: a tall brave Seneca, a broken wagon. Our mules, picking their way beside Uncle Peter's wagon, seemed at a loss without their traces or a wagon to pull. They would need to be fresh for their turn at what was now an encumbered wagon driven by Uncle Peter. Cotton, to save weight on the wagon, rode a mule behind the parade.

That night, much more tired with sore muscles we had not been used to working, we sat around our cook fire and discussed our choices again. Moses had ridden off on one of his evening sorties. Father was in favor of riding ahead to see whether a foundry could be found or a smith was in the area. Moses returned and reported a campfire and a wagon on the road an hour's distance. "We should come upon one another tomorrow," he said.

Father and Uncle Peter decided to wait till morning before riding to the other wagon to seek their knowledge of what lay west.

In the morning, before we had packed our bedding into Uncle Peter's wagon and hitched Father's mules, Father was back with good news. The oncoming wagon had told him there was a wagon works in South Bend, two days' drive west, which could repair axles. "If their wagon is any indication of the shop's quality, I'd say we have a good chance of replacing our axle," Father said, removing the pieces of our axle from the back of the wagon.

"I'll ride the axle to their shop," said Uncle Peter. "In the event this wagon becomes stuck, you are better without me than without Jesse." This was a sure sign to me that Uncle Peter had shrugged off all effects of the affairs in Marietta.

"That is fair," said father. "Wait for us there. Unless they have an axle that will do for us beforehand."

Father hitched the broken axle pieces to Uncle Peter's saddle, the small section in front across his saddle, the longer piece extending the length of his horse's right flank, above the stirrup. The horse could make good time and not have the pieces constricting his movements.

We waved goodbye to Uncle Peter, and I had one moment of panic, thinking of Ohio, but Uncle Peter seemed elated to be moving off at so much brisker a pace than we would manage. I wished it was my errand, not his. He was right, of course. Having only one hand, his most useful contribution was this ride to the rescue of our wagon.

Just before noon, the wagon Father had met came into view. A family that looked to be prosperous farmers reined up next to us. Their wagon, indeed, gleamed. New forged iron hubs and brass fittings for the cover, a brake pedal for both fore and aft axles, and a steering device that allowed for the front wheels to turn all the way underneath the wagon made our wagon look dilapidated. We admired the wagon and our hopes rose that our axle would be matched. "We saw your brother about two hours west, moving along easily. He'll be to the Studebakers by tomorrow, sure. They'll have the piece for you. Or make one up for you."

The farmers were duly proud of their means of transportation and praised the workmanship of the wagon makers, named Clement and Henry, the Studebakers. The farming family was working their way back east, breaking ground, planting and farming for settlers who were busy building or clearing, helping with harvests. We wondered why they would sign on as itinerant farmers rather than break their own ground. And why they had come west at all.

"We're not from Indiana," the wife offered. "We just thought it would be nice to see our old home in Philadelphia. We haven't been home since before the war."

I could agree with their feelings. It was my hope that we would deliver the sheep, stay with the Harrisons a seemly amount of time, a week or thereabouts, and then make it back to Esopus for Christmas. Without the sheep. It would be an easier passage.

We shared a noon meal with the travelers; then we set off after Uncle Peter for South Bend and what we hoped would be the salvation of our wagon.

When Uncle Peter was on his way to South Bend, I had moments of doubt that we would see him safe again. I did not want my good uncle to suffer any more unhappiness than he already had. But my worries left me the next morning as we set off after him.

We were following a map made for us by the family that had departed eastward. Our path would rejoin our old friend, the St. Joseph's River where it curved back from its northbound course. We would follow the St. Joseph's into South Bend.

We struck its tributary, flowing west, and by noon it broadened, and a collection of houses in an expanse of cleared fields marked the confluence of this tributary and the St. Joseph's. A woodcutter Father spoke to assure us the wagon manufactory was a thriving enterprise. He thought we might have to wait a few days because the number of wagons worked on and built was so great.

I began to find my curious side getting the better of me. What kind of shop would be so vital in this wilderness that settlers from all around would know if its fame?

We stayed one night in the field furthest west from the center of the settlement and our talk turned to the hardships faced by these settlers. Their fields were plowed around occasional boulders, rounded monuments of some giant's rock garden that even the strongest oxen could not budge. The soil was rich, and it would support their crops once they planted. One family spoke of their first cabin being washed away in a flood the previous spring, and their newly finished log structure was set on higher ground overlooking the St. Joseph where it cascaded over another boulder. Falling asleep to the sound of the water was peaceful and I dreamed of Black Creek and diving into the waterfall's basin. But I could not reach the basin in my dream. The falls rushed all around me but did not wash me into their pool, nor downstream.

In the morning, Moses and I swam in the St. Joseph's waters, only briefly though, for they were even colder than the St. Mary's had been. We reasoned they would be. The long day's drive to South Bend owed to our sheep's wanting to graze along the banks of the St. Joseph's. We had a time keeping them in motion, keeping the dogs on their job, and watching to see the wagon was on a firm roadbed.

It was truly a long morning, the warmest I could recall since Utica. During our noon rest, we encountered one wagon after another, some heading our direction, and even more going east. The road became a hard packed surface like the Cumberland Trail and widened as we arrived in South Bend. Moses and I crossed the flock to the opposite shore of the St. Joseph's River, and the sheep fanned out into the lush grass of a long, sloping embankment, grazing peacefully.

From our vantage point on the opposite shore, we looked across to a beehive of activity with wagons lined up outside a structure as big around as all of Ft. Wayne. Studebaker Wagon Works was ahum with forges and workers and hammered iron clangs. Wheels of various sizes were stacked along one wall. Evening was coming on, but traffic was as busy coming into the works as if it had been midday, when we arrived.

Father waved across to us, motioning us to come for our evening meal. We left the sheep in the care of the dogs and recrossed the river. Uncle Peter was nowhere to be seen, but Father told us he had arrived and was in a boarding house awaiting the completion of our new axle.

As we pulled on dry clothes, Uncle Peter sauntered to the wagon, looking handsome with a haircut and a new shirt. We were all to be supper guests at the boarding house, although since we were to take turns keeping the sheep, we would not stay in those comfortable boarding house beds.

South Bend was a hospitable town with no feeling of discomfort for Cotton or Moses or John Dark Sky. The territory had long since defeated the Indians, the Potawanamees, and most of their people had left this part of America. They left behind them some of the richest bottomland we had yet seen. If Wisconsin was anything like the farmland all around us in Indiana, it would be fine for crops and dairy livestock. The sheep would graze peacefully there if it was like the pasturing here. And I realized my thoughts were turned more to Wisconsin and to what it would be like and how it would be different from home.

XXVIII

MOSES AND I lay awake a considerable time that warm night listening to the water of the St. Joseph's River and watching the sheep quietly ruminate among the grasses leading down to the river. Our next three days would be our own here in South Bend, waiting with the sheep and Uncle Peter's wagon, while Father and Uncle Peter and Cotton went to rescue our wagon. A new axle was made ready the same evening we arrived at the Studebaker Wagon Works, and before dawn the three of them set off back to John Dark Sky to make the replacement. Our duty, to tend the sheep, was not demanding of our fullest attention and the distractions of the town of South Bend and the miracle of the Studebaker wagons was ours to enjoy.

But Moses was just as eager to ride off north to find the Michigan border, and so I spent the rest of the morning alone with the sheep and the dogs, simply watching the constant comings and goings at the wagon works. Not only were wagons being manufactured but also caissons for the transport of shells. A few three-wheeled machines with foot cranks, looking for all the world like man-powered chariots, were wheeled outside the factory beside a funny-looking carriage with no singletree for mules but instead a steam boiler mounted over the rear wheels. I watched the workers fire it up and saw it explode into clouds of steam each time its pressure passed a certain point. It caused a great stir and rather than being self-propelled, it repelled onlookers who scattered in all directions each time the steam escaped.

I was glad to be a safe distance away across the river from the steam carriage, but the three-wheeled man-powered cars were good playthings, and I wondered how to ask about them. Perhaps the works needed a test rider.

I kept coming back around in my mind to that three-wheeled cart. When Moses returned for the noon meal we were to take at the boarding house, I asked him what he thought of the idea of requesting a chance to test the three-wheeled machine. He had not crossed very far on his ride into Michigan, which he said was even flatter than Indiana, as far as he could see, and he brightened at the plan to ride the three-wheeler.

We examined closely the little chariots after dining. Three of the machines sat in a yard outside the wagon works together with a few two-wheeled versions that looked perilously unstable. The cranks were attached to the front axle and a steering bar was mounted to the forks that extended from the front axles.

I became aware of a bearded man in business attire and top hat standing behind us, watching us pour over the little carriages. I looked around as Moses was poking the steering bar. "Are you the owner?" I asked.

"You young men seem interested in the purchase of one of my velocipedes," he said. "My name is Clement Studebaker. Yes, I operate the wagon works here with my brother. Would you like to drive one of these?"

He must have seen the gaiety in our eyes as we introduced ourselves. "A pleasure to meet you, and a pleasure to try one, Mr. Studebaker," I replied. "How does one mount the velocipede?"

He laughed a deep chuckle from inside his enormous torso. "Here, let me show you," he said. And nimble as a cat, he threw one leg across the seat and pushed with his feet to start the three wheels rolling. His feet came up to the cranks as the wheels began to turn faster and suddenly he and the velocipede were off, wobbling down the road, dodging ruts and turning around in a short arc, pushing the cranks around until he was back even with me. He hopped off, breathing fast, and said, puffing, "Your turn, my good young man."

I took the machine by its steering bar and tossed my leg across the seat as he had done. Soon, I was pushing the ground under me faster than my legs would go and I reached my feet up to the spinning cranks only to veer into a rut and tumble off into the road, still grasping the steering bar. The machine, its wheels still spinning, was upside down on top of me.

Moses ran up and lifted the framework off my legs and said, "That was splendid. My turn." And he sprang onto the seat, propelling himself forward and pushing on the cranks in one motion, as Mr. Studebaker had. I ran along behind him breathing in the dust he kicked up. Moses turned and passed and was almost back to the wagon works and the watchful eye of Mr. Clement Studebaker when he put his feet down to stop his forward movement, and he toppled over right in front of the proud owner.

Mr. Studebaker snorted and picked up the velocipede, offering his other hand to the prostrate figure of Moses. If Moses was injured, he didn't show the least concern, but took the owner's hand and hopped onto his feet. "That's some frisky colt, Mr. Studebaker," he said. "May we ride her again?"

I caught up to them as Moses was asking this and heard Mr. Studebaker say, "Well, let me first show you the factory. Then we'll see what you two charioteers might want to do afterwards."

I could hardly believe our good fortune. Mr. Studebaker was to guide us through his wagon works. It was a treat so unlikely in this western wilderness state that my heart leapt in my chest. Moses ran ahead and I dusted myself free of the road still clinging to my pants and followed Mr. Studebaker past one huge forge with its bellows breathing as if giving birth. Away from the heat of the forge, we passed on into the center of the works.

Men in overalls were lifting a frame onto a chassis with the aid of an overhead block and tackle. Another team was bolting the frame of a completed wagon to its axles. Down the way, leading to a large storage barn, workers were pushing a third wagon onto a ramp.

Through the bay doors we peered down the ramp to the river where a flatboat with logs was being unloaded onto the bed of one of the sturdy wagons. A team or horses waited to be hitched to the wagon to take the load to the mill next door. Huge saws driven by waterwheel power from a spillway milled log and log. Mill hands stacked the sawn logs for the start of new chassis. The wagon works and mill were stimulating sights, and the noises inside were terrific.

Workers greeted Mr. Studebaker cheerfully, and he spoke to each worker in turn and got our names again and introduced us as his new assistants. "Come over to the bays, assistants," he called to us over the din. "I have one more thing to show you here."

Moses and I followed along into the dimly lit bay and saw a brightly painted green carriage with brass fitting and black leather seats that shone even in the darker part of the bay. "This is my pride and joy," he said, patting the spokes on one wheel. The wheel was rimmed with a substance that gave when I touched it, like the leather John Dark Sky had fashioned for our winter travel. "Rubber," said Mr. Studebaker. "It's made for wheels so the ruts and bumps in the road don't worry the rider. When you come for a ride with me, I'll show you the real comforts of travel."

"You could nail this around the wooden wheels on the velocipede," I said, pushing into the resilient surface of the rubber carriage wheel.

"One step behind us is all you are," Mr. Studebaker replied, "clever chap. We have made a few adjustments and we think we are onto one very sure way to attach a rubber tread to nearly any wheel. But our drivers have to test the wheel first before we build it for our carriage."

"When might we take you up on the offer of a ride?" Moses asked.

"What about tomorrow, that is if you are here for a few days. And I gather you will be, from what your uncle indicated."

"You sold him the axle to fix our wagon?" I asked.

"The word is 'offered.' I offered an axle," Mr. Studebaker said. "In return for which your Father offered to order a wagon."

"A new wagon? With those rubber wheels?" I asked, excited about travel in a lustrous vehicle like the one the itinerant farmers had.

"I might just have them," Mr. Studebaker said. "Looking ahead to when it will be built, next autumn, that is, I'd say we will have a few with the new wheel ready to roll."

"Next fall? But how will we get it? We're going to Wisconsin," Moses said.

"You will just have to come back for it," Mr. Studebaker said. "Now let's have us a little look at the foundry."

Moses and I did take the best ride either of us had ever taken, with Mr. Studebaker and his brother the next day. A phaeton, Mr. Henry Studebaker called it, with a team of horses the handsomest I ever before had seen, a high-stepping chestnut pair with braided tails and manes and brass tack. I squeezed the carriage horn and Moses got to apply the brake lever, which stopped the carriage smoothly on its rubber wheels. A softer ride I could not remember unless it was the raft we lay on in the lee of Esopus Island lazy summer days drifting in the Hudson River.

Moses and I spent the next two days riding the velocipedes and getting almost relaxed with the cantankerous three-wheeled machines. But when we tried the two-wheeled version, we both gave up after a few failed missions.

On one mission, I ran into a lady who stepped off the boardwalk to cross the road and I knocked her to her knees. When I tried to apologize, she laughed. She was not injured and she refused to allow me to dust her off.

"Nonsense!" she asserted. "What in the world is that anyway?" she asked, looking at the two-wheeled beast I was trying to tame.

"It's one of Mr. Studebaker's velocipedes," I offered, now speaking authoritatively.

"You wouldn't care to show my son how to operate it, would you?" she asked, adjusting her bustle.

"I wouldn't mind if he doesn't mind falling down a few times," I replied.

And so we offered a course of instruction to Mrs. Wright's son, a boy a little younger than me. He was a quick learner and even got the two-wheeler going a few hundred feet.

Moses did fall while showing him how to ride on the boardwalk and left some of the skin of his elbow and knee on a corner he was trying to navigate around. Board surfaces simply are not given to the likes of foot-powered machines.

We became the terrors of the town during those two days, I suspect. When Father's and Uncle Peter's wagons arrived late the third day, the town of South Bend must have breathed a sigh of relief. Mrs. Wright was sad to see us readying our wagon to move on. We were now getting into spring, and if we were to arrive in time to help with the Harrisons' field, we had better keep to our itinerary.

The Studebaker brothers were also sorry to see our family leaving. "We are losing our best assistants," Mr. Clement Studebaker said. "But we'll see you in the fall or winter for that wagon."

Father gave the Studebakers a note for forty dollars the night before we left so that the building of our wagon might begin. A sum that great must be getting us the likes of Mr. Studebaker's green beauty. Moses and I went back to say goodbye to Mr. Studebaker's grand carriage the morning we departed South Bend. I looked back from my horse as we rode beside the rails out of town. The wagon works was busy already as the sun rose.

"You look as if you might want to go back to South Bend soon," Father said. "What all did you and Moses do while we were away?"

"We became invaluable assistants for the Studebakers," Moses said. "I learned how to sell velocipedes. And Jess learned how to knock down ladies."

"Yes," I said from the other side of the wagon. "And Moses is ready to ride a velocipede to Wisconsin, except he doesn't grow skin fast enough to make it before he's skinned."

It was as if our wings were clipped to be back on the horses. But the wagon was fixed up proper, and we could look forward to our return in the winter. I hoped the snow would hold off so we could have another go at the velocipedes. Cranking the wheel in snow would indeed be perilous.

XXIX

Two long days west of South Bend, we marched the sheep through lush grasses waving in cool breezes, "coming from Lake Michigan," Father said. John Dark Sky had ridden ahead to the lakeshore and came back that second day.

Lake Michigan's shoreline was much like the shore of Lake Erie, but the dunes Moses and I climbed up and over to see Lake Michigan's waves were higher dunes, open to the steady winds blowing up the sides of the sandy slopes. Grass and vines grew on the lee side of the dunes, but sandy slopes all along the shores were swept bare up to their summits. We kept the sheep along the lee sides, but the wind carried sand into their fleece and coated the wagons and leather harnesses of the horses with grit. I tied my bandanna against my nose and mouth to keep the sand from getting into my throat.

Another flock of sheep was a day ahead of us. When we found their tracks in the sand, John Dark Sky and Moses rode ahead to see how many were being driven. They returned to report what we suspected, a much smaller number, twenty to thirty, and only two men on horseback with them.

We followed their tracks almost to Chicago, where they suddenly turned off, southward across a narrow railroad ridge that spanned a small river feeding into Lake Michigan. Our drive had followed the direction of the railroad from the spur out of South Bend to where it joined the main rails. We crossed the shallow water we found to be almost warm, and we led the sheep up the opposite bank and onward along the lakeside of the rails stretching out westward into Chicago. So we must have arrived in Illinois, the last state we would see before Wisconsin.

We continued on to the center of the town of Chicago. The railroad joined rails from two or three other directions. Yard hands in a switchyard as busy as Rochester's were unloading bags of grain for milling. Rougher cowhands from a western drive urged livestock down a ramp into a holding pen. Several passengers were disembarking as well.

Other wagons had the Studebaker insignia stamped on hubs and bearing other earmarks of the wagon works we remembered fondly. A phaeton like Mr. Studebaker's drove through the hubbub and came to a stop at the doors of a fishery on the lakeshore side of the tracks. A fancily dressed swell of a gentleman stepped out of the carriage, removed a top hat and gloves, and disappeared into the fishery.

"I believe he must be not far from his house," Moses said.

Cotton chuckled. Then he asked out loud, "I wonder if the fishery has a sturgeon."

But we passed without stopping to inquire. It was a busy day in Chicago. More than a dozen other carriages picked their way across the tracks and through the switchyard. Rail cars stood idle on sidings while a locomotive switched other waiting rail cars to and fro. It would not do to have the sheep amongst so much confusion for long.

Father remained in Chicago while we took the wagons farther north around the lake. We drove the sheep along the Chicago River and found a place to rest for the night along its northern shore where a bridge spanned the canal we were following. The canal would connect the Chicago River to another river west of us, the Des Plaines River, according to a workman.

The next day would be Sunday, and Father had not disavowed his thoughts about resting Sundays. Nor had Uncle Peter dismissed his resistance to resting Sundays. But we had not confronted a Sunday together since we left Columbus where we had not been laid up for repair of our wagon except for Easter Sunday, the week before our axle's breaking. Uncle Peter relented then, and we rested and had our eggs and Easter baskets and a day free from travel. When he joined us on the canal, Father brought back a leg of mutton for our Sunday dinner. He reported there was a Quaker Meeting in Chicago. He was insistent on our attending and bringing greetings from the Kingston Meeting. Uncle Peter agreed to remain with our sheep. Moses, Cotton and I would return to Chicago with Father to meditate the next morning at Quaker Meeting.

At dawn, Father shook us and told us to dress for Meeting. Moses was awake in a hurry, but I turned over in my blanket and must have fallen asleep again. When I awoke, Moses was squeezing water, cold water, out of his hair onto my face.

"The water is fine, sleeping beauty," he said. "But you probably need more beauty rest."

"Stop it!" I croaked, trying to cover my head with the blanket. But it was no use. I had to be up and dressed. I sat up and Father handed me a cup of hot coffee and sheep's milk. I sipped some and thanked him.

"We will set off for Meeting shortly, Jesse," he said. "You will be on your horse and ready then?" he asked.

"I am up," I said, raising up on one knee and trying to stand. But the sky spun around in front of my eyes and I sat back down.

"Jesse, are you not feeling well?" Father asked.

"Fine. I just feel tired still," I said, and got to my feet. But in truth, I was sick to my stomach and dizzy.

"Race you to the river," Moses challenged, knowing I liked to wash my face in cold water mornings.

He ran ahead. I wandered to the canal and knelt down. The sky wheeled me around again. I still had the mug of coffee in my right hand and drank some, but it tasted like a gun barrel. I put the mug down on a log and washed my face.

Moses called to me from the water. He was splashing around and waiting for me to come in.

I waved once and sat on the log in the morning sun.

Moses came up again, but he did not sprinkle water on me this time. "You look sick, Jesse. Are you sick?"

"I have a stomach ache and my head is hurting," I admitted.

"You are lucky," Moses said. "You may get out of going to Meeting."

And indeed, when Father saw me walking back from the river, he reached to my forehead and said, "You are feverish, son." He took a blanket from the wagon and wrapped it around me. "You will not be going into Chicago this morning. Stay warm by the fire and drink more while we are at Meeting. If you need anything, call your uncle or John Dark Sky. They will be here with the sheep.

Uncle Peter and John Dark Sky decided to take this day to shear the sheep. It was warm enough now to permit their wool to be removed and the sheep would travel more easily without the spongy wool pelts. We could sell the wool in Chicago the next day.

But I would be no help this Sunday. My head was pounding and I could barely rise to go to the wagon. I sat most of the morning, watching the sheep kick while John Dark Sky held them and Uncle Peter, grasping the shears in his one hand and parting the wool with his other arm, deftly clipped the mounds of wool from their backs and bellies.

When Father Moses and Cotton returned from Meeting, they joined in the shearing and soon bales of wool filled the back of our wagon. Moses, covered with lint, brought me a bowl of Scotch broth from their dinner.

"You missed the prettiest girls I ever did see at Meeting," he taunted.

"What good are pretty girls if you can't talk to them?" I squeaked, sipping broth. It tasted rich and was thickened with rice and the yellow gravy floating on top was seasoned with pepper and was tangy. I became aware of another flavor, an unfamiliar flavor in the broth, a grain-like taste that added to the broth's richness.

"I guess good-looking girls are no longer good enough for you," Moses replied.

"I think I shall shear Pricilla Hurd's braids for you when we get back," I said.

"Someone else may have done it for you before then," Moses said, and walked back for more of the flavorful broth. I finished drinking the broth and chewed the rice that seemed still to have its husks. I fell asleep and slept the rest of the afternoon.

By the time I could get up and take the boiling teakettle from the fire late that afternoon, all but one dozen of the sheep were sheared and back grazing in the field around our wagons. John Dark Sky was baling the rest of the wool and Moses was packing Uncle Peter's wagon with the bales. Cotton, combing fluffs of wool from his hair and clothing, took the kettle from me and poured it into a pot of coffee grounds.

"Would you like more of the soup from our dinner?" he asked.

"No, it was very good, thank you," I said. "I especially liked the brown rice you added."

"It was John Dark Sky, not I, who added the rice," Cotton said. "He was given the rice by an Indian trader who came along the river. You look better," he added, feeling my shoulder and forehead. "I believe your fever is gone."

"If I might have a cup of coffee," I said, "I would be grateful. I have a fierce thirst."

Cotton poured a mug of coffee for me and added honey and milk. Father had not taken the usual Sunday for rest. His exhausted face was deeply lined and he too was covered with bits of the gray wool. Even John Dark Sky looked worn. He and Uncle Peter had worked morning and afternoon. Their labors produced a wagon nearly full of baled wool and, from the looks of them grazing, a flock of much more comfortable sheep.

"The sheep look much smaller now," Moses said. I watched the sheep cropping the grasses and, indeed, the flock seemed smaller. Instead of the wall of gray backs, individual sheep stood out against the field. Each animal had a distinct shape, the larger rams standing out, the ewes and yearlings smaller between them.

We stayed sipping coffee until Cotton rose to carve the mutton leg he slowly roasted and turned during the night. He removed the spit and set the leg on a plank next to where I sat in the back of our wagon. Cotton whetted the carving knife and sliced the roast into thick slabs.

"Are you hungry, Jesse?" he asked when he handed me my plate.

The roasted meat looked good and I was feeling almost myself again. "Yes, the meat looks good." I took my plate and he placed a ladleful of brown rice next to the meat. John Dark Sky watched me as he took his portion.

"What kind of rice is this?" I asked him. We had not had rice since we cooked the last of a sack in New York, and here we were having it twice in one day.

"Thanksgiving," John Dark Sky said, reminding me of the wonderful feast in Lockport on the barge canal. "This is wild rice. It is only grown north of here. I have heard it spoken of but I had not before tasted it." He watched me put a forkful in my mouth as he ate from his plate.

"It is rice, certain, but not like any I ever tasted," I remarked. It had a groaty flavor and texture, and it was firm, the consistency of jerky.

We ate the rest of our meal, and between mouthfuls, we spoke of the next phase of our trip. Father said the Quakers recommended traveling across Illinois on this very canal to the Mississippi River. From there, we could follow the Mississippi north into Wisconsin.

Moses nodded approval of that route. "The Mississippi River, Jesse. I can show you the biggest river in the world. Even wider this time of year." He was excited.

Uncle Peter held out for a shorter northern path into Wisconsin. "Go along the canal and then up the Fox River." That was to have been our original route. "The Fox River flows from Wisconsin. Travel acrossland and through the state to the capital at Madison. From there, follow the Wisconsin River to Boscobel." He recited the course not even looking at the map Cotton spread on the ground.

I finished my plate of mutton and wild rice, every last grain, and spoke, perhaps out of turn, of what I recalled from my dream that afternoon while asleep in the wagon. "I believe there is a way like Uncle Peter's that is the shortest way and best for the sheep." And I knelt beside Cotton's map, using my fork for a pointer. "The shore of Lake Michigan is level and has ample pasture for the sheep. Let us follow it to here," and my fork fell on Waukegan, a town near the border with Wisconsin. It was as if I had no control over the movement of my hand or my words.

Then I lifted my fork from the map and spoke. "There will be a chain of lakes and streams with trails to lead the sheep through to the Rock River and to many lakes that surround the Wisconsin capital at Madison." I felt suddenly clear-headed for the first time all day. "Then we can follow Uncle Peter's course along the Wisconsin River."

Father looked at me and then at Uncle Peter and then at John Dark Sky. "Well, what do you think, Peter, John? Moses will be disappointed."

"You will take the Mississippi River back and come home your way, Moses," John Dark Sky said.

Father looked at me again. "Are you eager to return, Jesse?" he asked.

"We have to get Sarah and Ruthie," I said, turning to Cotton. "Cotton, certainly you will go back, and you will need someone, Moses and me, to go with you."

Moses spoke for the first time, having been surprisingly silent. "I would terribly much like to go along the Mississippi, but I believe John Dark Sky is right about waiting until we are on the way home. There might be floods this time of year that would make travel harder. In the fall, the river will be down and we can boat down to this canal."

"Well, it's decided then," Father said. "Tomorrow we go to the market in Chicago with all the wool and then follow the lake north. "Let us be sure we are rested well, and we shall pray now for and give thanks for our safety."

XXX

It was as if I had become an oracle. Moses quietly stayed around me rather than run into the river for his swim. Cotton refilled my coffee mug without asking. Only John Dark Sky treated me as usual. He unhobbled the horses and handed me the reins to take them for water. But even John Dark Sky waited until I returned and then went with me to hitch the mules to the wagon. Father offered me a hand up to the wagon seat to sit next to him for the morning departure to Chicago and the marketplace.

"How are you feeling, son?" he asked

"I am much better," I said, puzzled at all the commotion about a little thing like reading a map or being a little feverish.

I tried to puzzle it out and went through it in my head a few times with no luck. All the fever had done was leave me weak. I was fine otherwise. I would surely regain strength as the day wore on. With the solid food Cotton prepared. At least Shep behaved like the old Shep, running through the grass for the stick I threw. I decided to wait until nighttime to ask Moses about all this. By then it all might pass.

Monday morning at the market in Chicago was no less busy than it had been Saturday. All around our sheep, wagons were coming in from the country, carts pulled by oxen, packet boats towed to river berths. Locomotives both from north and south descending on the rail yard.

Not one half mile from the center of all this traffic were fields stretching down to the lakeshore road. Cotton and John Dark Sky remained at the wagon with our sheep. With Moses and me riding alongside and Father in the back loosening the bales of wool for inspection, Uncle Peter drove his wagon into the market.

"I imagine New York is no less busy than this," I said to Moses as we caught sight of the center of the market.

"It is this busy, no more," Moses replied. "But New Orleans goes on to more than five of this Chicago market."

We stopped at the bridge and watched more livestock driven from a railroad car, down a ramp and into a holding pen. Saturday's beeves were no longer in the pen.

Father stepped down from the back of the wagon when Uncle Peter stopped beside a woolen mill situated a bit farther down the Chicago River from the bridge. The bay doors to the mill stood open and two other wagons were unloading bales of wool. An inspector came up to our wagon and poked through the bales nearest the end. He wrote some figures down on a card and motioned to Father to enter the mill. Father disappeared inside, and when we peeked into the dark interior, we could just make out carding machines, winding the woolen thread onto giant skeins. Fibers floated everywhere in the gloom. Women with scarves around their fretful faces worked among the machines. I was glad to be outside. It made me uncomfortable to see into the mill.

Father returned and beckoned Uncle Peter to pull in through the bay doors. Mules and all, Uncle Peter hied into the dark woolen mill.

Moses and I waited until nearly noon, wondering when the wagon would return to the bright Chicago harbor sunlight. We explored the mariner's church and a boarding house where sailors were said to spend days waiting for their ships to load or be unloaded. No sailors were there on this Monday. Then we crossed the railroad tracks and walked along the broad beach, skipping stones and watching gulls follow a fishing trawler, its nets out where the river fed into Lake Michigan. Growing hungry, we recrossed the tracks past a stone water tower to find a bakery. We were about to enter a shop when Moses saw our wagon.

I waved and we ran over to the wagon. No bales of wool, and Father and Uncle Peter looked satisfied as they slowed to gather us in and drive on along the State Street side of the market. We rode along on the back of the wagon until it stopped beside a booth at the corner of Randolph Street. Father hopped down and bought three loaves of bread and a cheese. From an alchemist in another booth, he bought a bottle of green syrup. "Menthe de l'eau" Moses dubbed the liquid.

It would have been grand to stay all day in Chicago, but the sheep were waiting, newly shorn and eager to move on. Before we left Chicago, Uncle Peter bought a hat and boots. I tried a laceup boot, but mine still had some wear in them, so I decided to wait to ask for a pair until the fall.

It was mid-afternoon when we returned to see John Dark Sky bringing the sheep up from the river. We sat over bread and cheese, telling Cotton and John Dark Sky about all we had seen in Chicago. Then it was time to march the flock northward to Wisconsin.

As we set off north along the beach road, I thought no more about the sidestepping around me that plagued me earlier that morning. Whatever it was, and Moses insisted when we were skipping stones, that I was imagining things, whatever it was it had lifted by the evening.

Moses began to sing a hymn, "Amazing Grace" for no reason unless it was to celebrate the last month of our journey. With his high treble voice floating out over the sheep, Moses carried the melody. I joined him and Cotton picked up the harmony. On the third verse, Father and Uncle Peter sang too. The sheep, slim from their shearing, moved along the lake shore road keeping pace with the hymn sing.

We did not go far that evening even though a cool breeze was blowing in off Lake Michigan. The pasture we came upon in the small settlement of Wilmette was green and thick with grasses. We decided to stay there to prepare a meal, and then, since there was still an hour of daylight, to move on north until dark.

With our supper of cold mutton and bread and cheese, we drank some of the green mint syrup with cold lake water. The next hour along the lakeshore in the afterglow of sunset was like a painting of the Hudson River Valley. Tall trees waved in the breeze. Red leaf buds fairly glowed on maples, casting a glow over the sheep. The mule traces clacked and our wagons with their leather harnesses sounded like ships tied at dock in a gentle breeze. Moses began humming a melody Sarah used to sing, "Wade in the Water."

As darkness approached, John Dark Sky returned from the north and told of another pasture not far ahead. I wondered if it would be suitable, with all the glory we found already. It proved a fitting close to our day.

The small town, Winnetka, with a peaceful shoreline, gave us protection from thoughts of war and slavery and homesickness. A quiet and waning moon beckoned the others to sleep, but I felt refreshed by the day's events and stayed awake with Moses through his watch.

"I don't know what it is, but I am not the least sleepy," I said.

Moses yawned. "Well, then, you stay up and I can go to sleep." But he stayed awake with me and we talked about our favorite parts of the trip. "Mine is the market in Chicago," Moses said, ever the man for the moment. "What is yours?"

"Mine is riding up to the Lesters' field and seeing Uncle Peter's wagon, and Boca," I answered. "I was happy then as when Father returned from the war."

"I knew they would be there," Moses said. "I could feel it when we got close."

"How could you feel that?" I asked. "You never said a word."

"If I had said anything, it might not have come true," he replied. "It was nothing I saw or anything anyone said. Only a feeling I had."

"Well, if not saying anything helped bring it about, I'm glad," I said. "By the way, why were you so especially generous to me this morning and in Chicago?"

"I never paid you extra favors this morning," he said. "You must have dreamed it. You were still sick. You got better when we were at the market."

"No, it was all of you, not just you. Father and Cotton and even John Dark Sky a little. All of you were something, almost afraid of me. Something."

Moses was silent. He started to say something, and then thought better of it. Finally he said, "Jesse, you were feverish last night. What you said made no sense at all. We could understand nothing of what you were saying."

"I said to take this route, just as we are taking it. You remember, don't you? I pointed with my fork."

"You just sat looking into the fire and barely eating your food," Moses said. "We are taking this road because the Indian met with John Dark Sky and told us about it."

"No. I did. I know what I said, Moses."

"You dreamed you said it maybe," he countered. "John Dark Sky pointed it out with a stick. You spoke, but it was gibberish, and then you just sat staring at the fire."

We were quiet a while. Then I asked, "Did I not say anything about this road along Lake Michigan?"

"That was John Dark Sky," Moses said.

XXXI

I must have dosed off towards sunrise. Cotton's baking sourdough bread and coffee woke me, and birds chirping overhead reminded me that this was a day to write up. Sometime today we would enter Wisconsin.

Excited as Moses and I were, we realized we would probably not even know where exactly among the uncharted lakes, the division between Illinois and Wisconsin lay.

Lakes dotted the woods trail from Waukegan to the Fox River, a lacework of streams and marshes with waterfowl more plentiful than I could remember in New York. It seemed as if more water than land lay in our path. Insects swarmed over the water and black flies peppered our faces. Making our way through the watery, low-lying marshland took all the patience we could muster.

But we were eager to get on, to be in Wisconsin. Finally, we arrived at a river we thought to be the Fox River, flowing swiftly southward. We followed it north until it broadened out into a lake. This was the lake we thought must border Wisconsin.

Although we were not certain, we gave thanks on the lakeshore for our safe passage thus far.

"Father, we thank Thee for Thy many benefits," Father said in a quiet voice. "And, if it would not be asking too much, we would be grateful for a peaceful and safe journey to our destination. Amen." We were all, even the sheep, too tired from the morning's trek to complain when Father signaled to move on around the western shore of the lake. He finally stopped to rest where the stream narrowed once again. We partook of a longer evening meal than usual, and then we bedded down for what sleep we could. My watch was the last, and before it had ended with the sunrise, we were up and moving again. We would not have time to become lazy in Wisconsin.

The Wisconsin countryside was lush grassland. In some fields, cattle and deer grazed alongside one another. Tall, virgin growths of oak and elm stretched above the other trees bordering fields, and broad beech or apple trees occupied the center of many clearings.

All afternoon, I rode along expecting to be overcome by some triumphant feeling. The slow movement of the tiring flock and the gentle sway of our wagon through the trail we were following west were, if anything, no different from the sensations of traveling through Indiana or Illinois. Except for the fine weather, we could be in any of the states we had crossed. I began to long for home.

We stopped for our evening meal as the sheep passed in and out of shadows of the tall trees. I expected Father and Uncle Peter to bed down for the night here, in the canopy of pale green leaves just budding out overhead. But they rose after our meal and Father bid Moses and me gather the dogs to continue along with the flock till dark. It was as if now that we were in Wisconsin, we would need less rest. I began to wonder if we would be stopping for the Sabbath in two days.

If we began to wonder too whether we would be traveling all night, our fears ended as we arrived at the shore of another idyllic lake. We rolled out our bedding on the sandy shore and slept under a warm night sky. A crescent moon was cradled in the soft water of the lake.

In the morning, Moses and I swam out as far as was safe in the cold water and ate heartily when we dried off and dressed. Father and Uncle Peter seemed not as rushed to move away from this spot. The lake held us all in a thrall with the clear reflections of its pines on the smooth surface waters.

Our path went through hilly country down to the shore of another lake, even larger and more magical than the lake whose waters we had slept beside all night. We circled this new lake, a long path around its southern shore, and let the sheep follow a river flowing west. This third night in Wisconsin we camped along the river, a branch of the Rock River we learned, awaking to the crash of fish after mayflies. In frenzied rushes, fish frantically broke the surface to devour the hundreds of pale green flies that had hatched overnight. We could not catch any of the fish on our lines, not even when Moses waded in and tried to scoop them up in his hat.

It was time to gather the flock for our day's travel when I gave Moses my hand and he climbed the banks of the river. He dressed and breathed with an exhausted sigh, "Northern fish are harder to land than Southern fish."

As he shook his head to dislodge water from one ear, I laughed and said, "Maybe Northern fish are just smarter, Moses."

XXXII

All along the broader main branch of the Rock River, we urged the sheep to move with sprightlier steps. It seemed the flock sensed our dawdling. In their own way, the sheep were captive to the same spell that had Moses and me transfixed. It was only with supreme effort that we arose, dressed, ate, and herded the sheep those first three mornings in Wisconsin.

We passed another lake brimming with fish, jumping after more of the mayfly nymphs. It would have been heavenly to sit and watch them all day, but we turned northward again, and the lake fed into a streambed that led us all the way into Madison.

Wisconsin's capitol was a new building and seemed grander than the structure's size indicated. But it was nowhere near as handsome as the capitol in Columbus.

The sheep moved slowly past the college buildings and the school and church, and seemed to stop altogether at the base of a hill that overlooked a large lake. While Moses and John Dark Sky and I set up camp, Father and Cotton and Uncle Peter went back along State Street for provisions. With the camp set at the base of the highest hill in town, Moses and I rode our horses to the hilltop and enjoyed a cool breeze coming off the lake as we kept watch on the sheep below.

It was my idea to ride out to a point of land stretching into the lake, but Moses pointed out that we had to watch the sheep. One of us could go out to the point and the other could be shepherd if any sheep strayed from the hillside. We played rock, scissors and paper to see which of us would ride out along the peninsula and I won.

I rode down the hill and along the lake until it arched out onto the spur of land extending away from the shore. The trail became no more than a path, and the horse was reduced to a walk. The lakeshore was visible no more. A house stood empty on the point leading into the lake with a dock leading to the remains of a boathouse. A wherry was upturned beside the boathouse on skids. Its copper rudder, blackened from lack of use, lay beside it and weeds grew up around. Perhaps the boat's owner had gone off to the war; perhaps the family had moved elsewhere. I hoped the rowers would return to this lake to slide the boat again out on its surface. I hoped I would set the raft out along the Hudson River's currents again soon.

When I was halfway back, Moses came running along the path. "We are going to stay today and attend services at the church tomorrow," he said.

"Good. The big house at the end is worth seeing. Hop on and come back with me." And I turned back to the house, with Moses behind me. At the boathouse we sat on the boat and watched fish surfacing off the point. "Some spirit may be protecting the house," I said, "or we might go inside. It's often that way with grand houses that are idle."

"Maybe each person who comes here becomes a protector," Moses suggested. "The house shows no sign of being disturbed."

"What do you think? That the owner was killed in the war and his family gone to collect his remains?"

"No, they would have sent for them," Moses said. "No, I believe the house was never lived in. It looks newly built." Moses rapped the boat's laths. "And this boat looks little used. Maybe the owner died shortly after he built the house."

"Or maybe his wife died and he could not bear to live here longer," I said. But both of us felt there had been a loss here, that something or someone was missing and would not return.

We walked our horse along the point and watched a sailboat turn away across the lake and disappear into the shoreline's shadows. The late afternoon sun glinted off the water like a shield. We went back to the house and rode to where we saw our flock along the lakeshore.

From the hill overlooking the lake that evening, we saw the forested point of land we had visited, but the boathouse was around the corner, hidden by trees. The great house also was hidden. Another sailboat plied the surface of the lake.

Madison stood in from the shore, along State Street. The town lay between this lake and another we had passed earlier on the Rock River. We felt as if we were floating between two bodies of water, that the capitol building was a boat that had landed on an undiscovered shore.

"Do you ever feel as if we were on a voyage, not a sheep drive?" I asked Moses.

He did not have the same feeling, but he did feel that we were discoverers, "Columbuses, or who were they who came to Wisconsin through the St. Lawrence River into Lake Michigan? Samuel de Champlain and Jacques Cartier?"

We could not be sure, and neither Father nor Uncle Peter could remember. "But," Father said, "there are French names in these parts. Prairie du Sac will be where we join the Wisconsin River the day after tomorrow. And we are near towns called Belleville and De Forest. The French explorers and trappers were here and all the way along the Mississippi River to New Orleans. You know that, Moses, and that French is still spoken in Quebec although the British control it.

"And," Father went on, "some Confederates feel it might have been better if the French still controlled New Orleans. The Union Army would not be there if France still owned Louisiana."

"Why did the French not side with the South?" I asked.

"The French and all other countries will have to wait until this war is ended," Father said. "It is not proper to side with one warring party in civil strife not of one's own country. But if a foreign power attempts to overtake another, as the British did in our Revolution, then France lent aid justifiably."

XXXIII

Sunday morning in Madison, Wisconsin was quiet. Bleating sheep were the only sounds of the early day. From the top of the hill, Moses and I saw the first churchgoers arrive in their carriages. We were to attend the service that morning, and so we climbed up on our horse, and I turned him down the hill to meet with Father, Cotton and Uncle Peter and go to Wisconsin Sunday morning worship.

The Congregational Church was crowded and the choir sang out forcefully. There was an offering of communion, and the entire congregation was invited to partake. So we all drank our wine from the thimble-sized cups, and at the small croutons that served as symbols of the body of Jesus. Since we were Quakers, the divinity of Jesus did not enter into the elements of communion for us. But I must have kept some of my early religious sentiments. I felt our entire trip had been ordained, somehow, and that ours was a religious mission. I don't know how I could have come to feel that way. That wasn't the case Christmastime at the Presque Inn. Father's insistence that we stop every Sunday must have had an effect on me.

During the church service, I whispered to Moses, "Do you have the feeling that our trip is a pilgrimage?"

He gave me a startled look and said almost aloud, "Yes. You know I felt that all along. You mean to tell me you are thinking that way finally?"

"I'm not sure," I mumbled. Then I wrote on the back of a guest card, "If we have come this far and been through so much, does God's purpose exist in all of this?"

Moses looked at what I wrote. "That is all your father has been trying to say."

A family with two older sons who sat next to us in church invited us to have a stay with them, and Father accepted. They had cleared a farm 40 miles west of Madison, and when they saw our encampment on the hillside, they invited us to pick up and move to their pastures. The older son, David, explained the husbandry lessons he was studying and the courses in classics and other classes in letters and sciences. One of the younger son's roommates had attended private boarding schools in Massachusetts and was interested in our Quaker school.

We agreed to bring our sheep to their farm on the river by the next Wednesday.

After the worship service and the social hour, while Cotton prepared our dinner, I wrote what had been running through my mind at church. I wrote what Moses and I whispered to each other and what I wrote on the guest card. I wrote about the sermon the minister spoke, most of which I couldn't remember, but one thing he said stood out and I put it down. He read about faith being like a mustard seed and how it grew to move a mountain. After I wrote that, I sat on the shore of the lake and decided to make the mustard seed the idea of our journey and to make the mountain the long trip itself that we were moving through. I don't know if I made a right relating of the Bible passage to our shepherding journey, but I felt calm while I gave it more thought as I sat by the water and reflected on it.

The next morning we hitched the mules to the wagons and herded the sheep around the lake past the point Moses and I explored. I felt a new meaning in each routine chore. Rounding the sheep into a flock was an important act. It was not as if our destination only would prove the worth of the journey. The journey itself was its own reward. These were fine sheep, and our dogs had been faithful beyond all cause. The wagons were sturdy and needed only one repair of any significance. Food was always plentiful, and here we were going to share a day or two with a Wisconsin family we would not have come to know if we had not been on such a journey.

We had brushed against the worst kinds of evil in the guise of Union soldiers, but we had won out against them. We would not have learned about them if we had not been on this trip. There had been so much more good than there had been ill. How could we have learned how best to combat the evil if we had not experienced it? We might never have learned to recognize intolerance and how to register our distress over intolerance.

As our trip wended farther west, it, the trip itself, became what we had been seeking. Everything that was important, everything that we had learned, was in the going. The fine families, brave settlers, and generous innkeepers, harsh canal boaters and hard-working mill hands, and all the other travelers along our way, they were parts of what we had learned. Morgan's Raiders too were part of what we had come to know. With what we hoped were but six days of travel remaining, the last part of our sheep drive, we would, each one of us, discover what the ending of the trip would teach us. There was still that to experience.

Our arrival west of Madison at the newly plowed farm, ready for spring planting, was to be our final partaking of hospitality from a family until we would arrive at Boscobel. The Lloyd-Joneses had come along the Wisconsin River past Dodgeville to farmland that Mrs. Lloyd-Jones' brother claimed a dozen years before. Like our trip, theirs had brought sheep across country from New York, and now their flocks numbered over three hundred. They also raised dairy cattle, and, from the smell that greeted us as we brought the wagons around to their barn, a considerable poultry population too.

We were welcomed warmly into their farmhouse. The Lloyd-Joneses' two sons who were attending college at Madison also spent weekends working on the farm during planting. Their rooms were filled with books in Latin and Greek as well as architectural texts and Shakespeare plays.

It was the first time I had thought much about our Quaker school for a considerable time, and it made me all the more wishful that I could be back in classes. This was the time of year that made going to school best – the trees in bloom along the carriage path leading into the school building, newly mown fields for games, girls in pinafores and some in the dusters we had begun to see the year before. And the lessons would be coming to an end with the most interesting part being the tests to determine what we would be studying the next year, who would pass and who would have to repeat the subject matter. It was always the time I felt I learned the most.

But I had learned so much else on our journey. It would be hard to return to a classroom and a schedule. I would forever be torn between the life of books and the life of the open road where adventure lurked around each turn in the river.

We passed a pleasant day with the Lloyd-Joneses. The next morning, when we set off west to follow the southern shore of the Wisconsin River to Boscobel, I felt I brought many of their interests and ideas with me. The sheep moved among the clumps of grass, already high in places, and through the plowed fields on both side of the river road. The Wisconsin farmers were industrious, and not a few were out planting already, like the Lloyd-Joneses.

Just before sunset after we had dined on the wonderful cold venison meal the Lloyd-Joneses put up for us, we came to a bend in the Wisconsin River. To the north, the river spread out into a wide lake. Here, on the shore, it wound through fields that were planted well enough back from its flood waters so as not to come awash, but near enough to be irrigated if there came a dry spell.

Father brought our wagon alongside Uncle Peter's and we set the sheep out to pasture along the banks of the river where we camped. The sheep grazed until dark and then gathered under several of the willows that bent down to the river's edge.

Moses and I took the first watch and wondered whether the Harrisons' farm would be like those here, along the river. "If it bears any resemblance to the Lloyd-Joneses' farm or any of those we passed, it will be a prosperous farm indeed," I said.

Moses agreed. "In Esopus, if your father and your uncle Peter had had one-half of the rainfall Wisconsin has, the field down to the river would be greener than these even."

"Or if the Hudson River ran as level with our field, then troughs could be dug to the fields to offset the drought," I added. "Father often wondered whether it might be done."

"It is best to respect his river, if it floods like the Mississippi," Moses cautioned. "Too much water is worse than none at all."

"There's good and there's bad in both rivers," I said. "But I declare, these waters pass through the richest land we have yet seen."

"Wait until we see the Mississippi," Moses said, always his song, and now the chorus of these waters so near his great river gave the song more meaning.

Once again, I could not sleep when Father relieved us. Moses too was wakeful. Father was resigned to have us stay up with him and talk and watch the sheep beneath the willows.

"We have another two days along this river," Father said, "and the third day we shall arrive in Boscobel. God has been truly generous to us on the trip. Our long march will soon end. New work awaits us. Clearing fields, and plowing likely, and planting."

"And may we go to the Mississippi River when we finish and the seed is in?" Moses asked.

"It may we shall go then. If not, then after harvest," Father said. "In the meantime, this is a fine river, this Wisconsin River. You might try fishing it waters now. John Dark Sky heard said from the Lloyd-Joneses of a fish called a sauger, a perch but much larger, that has the tenderest flesh next to trout. And it feeds at night."

That was all we needed. Moses brought out the poles and I collected worms from the grasses by the river. Soon from the overhanging branches of the willows, we were dangling our lines.

Less than an hour from the moment we first lowered the lines, I brought up a big fish, four or five pounds, its orange fins and dorsal fan spread out, creamy eyes glowing in the moonlight. "This must be one of the saugers, Moses," I said excitedly.

Moses leaned across the branch where I stretched the fish. "It must be; it's too large for any perch. Let's keep it and try to catch a few more."

John Dark Sky grinned to see us back fishing when he came to relieve Father. "You will have good luck in the river," he said.

"I swear, he can smell the fish in a stream or lake," I said to Moses.

"I'd allow he can see them too," Moses said. In the next hour, Moses brought up two fish like mine, and that was enough for a fine breakfast for all of us. Then came the false daylight that sends all night feeders back to the depths.

True daylight found our caravan moving again, along the Wisconsin River. I rode among the sheep. The land rose to a high ridge overlooking the river. Mountains lifted to the north, across the river. Clouds hid some of the summits. The ridge where we stopped the second night made Moses and me homesick for our farm and for the Hudson River. The shore of the river was one hundred feet below us with a slope down to its banks like our hillside pasture in Esopus, and railroad tracks passed near to the shore here too. It was so like being home I almost cried. We said our customary prayer for the wellbeing of Sarah and Ruthie. And for the first time, my prayer for a safe return to them seemed closer to being realized.

"I feel as though Sarah and Ruthie are here with us," Moses said when we had settled into our blankets.

"It is so like our farm," I said. "I can't help but think they are here too, somehow."

"Do you think they will ever see this country?" Moses asked.

"I don't know. It could be. But not until Ruthie is older."

"She would have to be our age to be of any help," Moses said.

"Traveling with a young person would be harder truly," I said.

"If they come, I hope they pass well north of the Ohio River," Moses said.

Clouds surrounded our morning watch, casting gray mist down to the river and concealing the sheep. We waited to gather the flock until the fog lifted enough to see more of them. Here and there the dogs emerged with a few strays. We kept between the rails and the river, moving westward on our last day to Boscobel. During our noon meal, the fog finally blew away, up over the hills that rose now almost from the edge of the rails and emerged out of the cloud cover.

Moses rode ahead with John Dark Sky, as he did so many times in Indiana. "Maybe I'll get to Iowa across the Mississippi," he called as he trotted away in John Dark Sky's wake. Before we had even begun to gather the flock and return to our journey, Moses galloped back to us, waving his hat and hollering to wake the dead. "Boscobel!" he shouted breathlessly. "Boscobel!" he gushed again when he rod alongside our wagon. "It's there. Yonder!" And he pointed downriver to a steeple we could just make out rising out of the valley along the river. If we had known to look, we could have seen it when the clouds cleared.

"Before we begin our last hours, let us pray," Father said. We all took off our hats, and Moses stopped panting and climbed down off his horse as Father knelt and prayed. "Almighty Father, we give our humble thanks for delivering us this day to our long sought destination. Enrich the lives of those whom Thou hast brought us aid, and bless those who are far from us, as Thou hast blest us." And then he added before we could say amen, "And bring us safely back."

Back? To Esopus? Or from Esopus here again. Which back? Father did not say, but it was not worrisome to me then. I was too happy to be within sight of the town to which we had come from such a far place.

Father brought his uniform tack and parade hat out from the trunk attached to the side of our wagon. Uncle Peter did the same. This was to be a formal entrance if ever there was one.

We headed the flock and turned our wagons west along the river one last time and came down into the town. We were about to inquire at a livery where the Harrison spread was when we heard a commotion down the road leading from the river. Father stood up on the wagon seat and shaded the sun from his eyes. "Hurry!" he pointed to us. "They have a rifle aimed at John Dark Sky!"

Moses turned the reins and dug his heels sharply into the horse's flanks. I turned Boca and caught Moses and passed him and galloped up to the small knot of townspeople. Men were gathering around a man with one leg who was supporting a rifle with a crutch under his arm. The rifle was pointed at John Dark Sky.

"Wait!" I shouted as Moses rode up beside me. "That's John Dark Sky and I am Jesse Stiles and this is Moses," as if those names meant anything at all to the man.

The men in the back of the circle between us and John Dark Sky turned to see Cotton, who was approaching on his horse, and then to look at a wagon and flock of sheep in the background coming down the road into their town.

I was not aware of danger as I jumped off Boca and ran through the circle of townspeople and up to stand beside John Dark Sky. "Are you Lieutenant Harrison?" I gasped at the man holding the rifle.

He looked at me and then glanced up. As the crowd parted and Father's wagon drew close, the sheep fanned out behind, Lieutenant Harrison stared at the man sitting on the wagon seat, wearing a Union Army dress hat and jacket. I have never seen a man so at a loss as Lieutenant Harrison.

A woman came down porch stairs and through the gate to the farmyard where the crowd had gathered, patting her brow with a bit of bunting. "You say Stiles?" she asked looking not at me but at the wagon just drawing to a halt outside her front gate.

"Lieutenant Frederick Harrison," Father called from the wagon seat. "I declare a truce. My man is Mr. John Dark Sky. And may I introduce my brother Major Peter Stiles and his aide, Mr. Cotton Manners. And those in front of me, my son Jesse and his friend Moses Manners."

"Colonel Stiles," the man finally managed, lowering his rifle absently. "My Stars! I am thunderstruck."

Fred and Helen Harrison were still stroking the sheep and looking over the wagons as Father and Uncle Peter began to unload the whale oil and unhitch the mules. "And when a native came to the window as I was sewing," Helen Harrison said, shaking her head, "it was so unnatural of me, but I was so surprised I shouted and Fred went for the rifle."

"It's a good thing your man didn't run," Fred Harrison said after we had taken supper around the large table in their dining room. "I might have done something I'd have been sorrier for than anything."

"Yes," Father said, sipping from his stein of the Harrisons' beer. "But you held."

"We have so many friendly Indians in town, trading and trapping for us, I do not know what came over me," Helen Harrison said again. "I fear for little Frances' safety I reckon. But I can't believe you are here. Fred said you'd be coming, but I never expected you would actually come with a whole flock of sheep all that long distance. Now tell us all about the travels."

The lack of sleep and the sudden diminishment of all our duties set in upon first me, then Moses. Mrs. Harrison noticed our discomfort and said, "You men must be pretty near ready to drop. I'll arrange the bedding in the loft for you and you may go right up."

Moses was asleep before the candlewick had ceased to glow. I tried to write a little in my journal about our arrival, but there was too little moonlight even from the dormer where I lay looking out on the sheep. I lay down the journal and tried to think what I would write in the morning. It was hard to say what the trip meant. It had ended. Would I ever find its true purpose?

I lay awake most of the night, not sleeping, just watching the sheep. I was tired beyond sleep. Tears washed my eyes when the first light grayed the Boscobel sky. The sheep were clustered around the hay that someone, Father probably, had forked out for them. Father was up and had almost unloaded our wagons into the Harrisons' barn. So perhaps I had slept, for I was stiff and cold and it was light out. I wrapped the quilt Mr. Harrison gave me tighter around me and watched the sheep move slowly around their new pasture. Moses would be awake soon and we could take them down to drink the water of the river.

Made in the USA
Lexington, KY
18 March 2016